G.O.D.: GOLD, OIL AND DRUGS

A novel by Saleem Little

GOLD, OIL AND DRUGS

Mitanni Publishing
A subsidiary of Mitanni Enterprises LLC
PO Box 13099, Harrisburg, PA 17110, USA
Copyright ©2012 by Saleem Little

Cover Design by Saleem Little

G.O.D.: GOLD, OIL AND DRUGS

A

The Prologue

Buffalo, Ny 1986

It's the year of Reaganomics and major political scandal. Crack cocaine is still in its infant stage but has already caused major increases in the number of emergency-room visits, drug-related arrests, and infant mortality as a rash of "crack babies" are being born in every ghetto across America. A grinding level of poverty and homelessness is rampant and its effects are being felt nation-wide. Eric B. is the unofficial president and Rakim is his spokesperson. The price of oil is on the verge of crashing and the Reagan administration is plotting to sacrifice domestic oil producers in order to win the "Cold War" with Russia. And while oblivious to the world of politics and the true dynamics of the poverty in which he lives, Wally is just trying to survive, a most difficult task considering the obstacles.

Wally walks slowly up the cracked steps that lead to his decayed apartment building. Its bland-gray paint and decaying exterior reflect the depressing mood you feel as soon as you see it, or even worse, once you step inside. Wally hates coming home to this place. His mother, which Wally thinks is too magnanimous a title for the woman, is addicted to free-basing cocaine and is always too high or too drunk to recognize her son's wants or needs. It seems as if poverty becomes a multi-faceted problem that affects not only one's financial status, but eventually leads to an impoverished deficiency in morals, work ethic and compassion. The saddest part was that Wally always felt that the state of poverty he and his mother lived in could have easily been overlooked had it been compensated by love.

Wally opens the door to his tenement slowly, peeks inside, and sees that his mother is in her normal position. It is a sight he has come so accustomed to seeing that had she not been in a deep sleep with her arms and legs dangling from the couch he would have thought something was wrong. Wally shakes his head in disgust at the sight of her withered breast hanging out of her bra. Not only is it a part of her anatomy he shouldn't be seeing, it was a stark reminder of what the drugs had done to her. All of her tattered clothing now hung from her skeletal body; scarred by years of abuse and rapid weight-loss.

From his position in the doorway, she actually looks like a skeleton in a comatose state. Nearly every bone in her cadaverous body is visible through her thin, ebony skin. Her mouth hangs wide open as a house fly dances from lip to lip; taking an intoxicating sip of the Old English on them every time he lands. If it wasn't for the occasional snore, and the steady rising and falling of her emaciated chest, you would think she was dead.

Her hand hangs off the couch and it has knocked over an empty beer bottle, and right below her fingertips is a gray, smoke-stained glass pipe. Wally wonders why she is sleep, base usually has her wide awake, wired, with her permanently blood-stained eyes, opened wide. Then he remembers she's been up ten days straight; no shower, no bath, and very little sleep. Just running the streets on her coke binge, stealing, prostituting, and God only knows what else. The T.V. momentarily distracts Wally. He tunes in for a split second to hear what the reporter is saying.

"The pervasive poison of illicit drugs continues to course through the nation's bloodstream, damaging or destroying everything in its wake and making it the most enduring and serious internal crisis this nation has faced since the Civil War."

Sarcasm washes over Wally's face as he says,

"You think?"

Wally covers his nose to block out the foul, death-like stench that's seeping through her filthy pores like toxic fumes. It's mixed with the stink of the apartment which smells like a dead body is decomposing in the closet. He tip-toes lightly, trying desperately not to wake her, knowing that if he does she'll find something, anything, to fuss at him about. She'll probably tell him to clean up all the trash that she has thrown all around the small, compact apartment. Dirty clothes, pipes, beer bottles, spilled ash trays, three-day-old dishes with disease-infested cockroaches crawling all over them.

"Forget that." he thinks as he sneaks into the kitchen and opens the refrigerator.

The hinges creek.

"Damn" he curses quietly, wanting anything but to wake the zombie - as he now refers to her.

Finally, he opens it...nothing! In the bare refrigerator is a week old, half-full, 40-ounce of Old English, a box of Arm & Hammer baking soda, and a pot of badly molded pork and beans that smells like a sewage drain. He quickly puts the lid back on the pot of pork and beans. He keeps glancing over his shoulder at his mom. He has now reached the point where he dreads any form of interaction with her.

"OK, here we go." Wally says as he plucks a hungry roach off of a pack of bologna. The roach scurries to the sink and Wally rinses off a piece of bologna. He eats it slowly, trying to savor the near-spoiled taste, knowing this will have to last him for a minute, at least until he gets to Dumare's house or to the store to steal something, whichever one comes first.

The running water wakes the zombie. Wally's mother has earned this nickname because she always reminded him of those brain-eating creatures in the cinema. Though alive they appeared dead and this is how his mother now appeared to him. Her skin was pale and emaciated and she stalked for her prey, cocaine, at night like a zombie for brains. She resembles a zombie even more so as she wakes up out of her sleep like a zombie rising from its grave. Wally quickly gobbles up the rest of the bologna. She will try to take it from him if she knows it's the last piece. Everybody in this small, run down, one bedroom apartment is in a struggle for their pitiful lives, from the roaches and mice, to mother and son. This battle for food is the norm.

"What you doin in that 'frigerator boy?"

She asks as if Wally has committed a crime by feeding himself.

"You's a greedy lil nothing..."

She speaks with such a seething disdain for Wally. He has no idea where the hatred comes from. Besides her self-hatred, it stems from the disapproval of his deceased father. In her eyes, Wally's father was to blame for the position they were in now.

Wally ignores her. This is a new skill he's learned, he's only ten but he's smart enough to know that she's no mother. He knows that just giving birth to a child doesn't make a woman a mother. A mother loves the child she gives birth to. She cares for and about it, consoles it, guides it and nurtures it when it is sick and lonely. A mother doesn't just deliver a baby into this cruel world and leave it to fend for itself. A mother was supposed to be the child's first protector and her everlasting love was supposed to last a lifetime. This wasn't the case with Wally and the Zombie. So now, to stop him from caring he blocks her out. She only exists when he gives her attention.

Wally quickly walks past her and to the door he just crept in not even two minutes ago. Lately he never stays home too much longer than that.

"You hear me talkin' to you boy?!"

Wally slams the screen door; it smacks the frame so hard the latch doesn't catch and the door flings back open.

"Get back in here and clean up this God damn house!"

He hears her screaming, ignores her, and her screams continue, fading gradually as he runs toward his best friends' house. He's left wondering why the only time his mother ever discusses God is when she's cursing. He shakes the thought as the feeling of joy begins to fill him as he gets closer to Dumare's house. In Wally's eyes, Dumare's house was to him, what that old attic was to Ann Frank; a Safe Haven.

Dumare stands nervously in front of his father who is asking him to recite a lesson verbatim. The lesson he's reciting is a degree in his One-twenty, the curriculum taught to Five-Percenters. He begins slowly than stutters. It's not that he can't recall the lesson; it's just that his father, a devout Five Percenter named Curtis, has an imposing presence and intellect about him that naturally intimidates people. This effect is ever present now as he quizzes his youngest son.

"Start again, the first degree in your student enrollment." He says in his trademark, non-negotiable tone. Dumare takes a breath then starts again:

"Who is the Original man? The original man is the Asiatic black-man, the maker, the owner, the cream of the planet earth, the father of civilization and God of the universe."

Curtis smiles proudly.

"Alright now let me hear the 16th degree in the 1-40 and tell me how they coincide."

Dumare smiles, he loves to make his father proud. His confidence kicks in and he begins to recite his lessons effortlessly:

"Who is the five percent on this planet? Poor, righteous teachers who do not believe in the teachings of the ten-percent, for they are all wise and know who the true and living God is, and who teach that the Almighty true and living God is Allah, the Supreme Being, Black man from Asia, and teach freedom, justice and equality to all human families of the planet earth; otherwise known as civilized people, also Muslims and Muslim sons."

With dignity Dumare goes on to explain to his father that the first degree is the truth that the sixteenth degree is speaking of and what the five percent teaches and adheres to.

Again, Curtis nods in approval, knowing that at nine years old, his son is precocious. The luminous glow in Dumare's household is a stark contrast to than ominous shadows that encompassed Wally's.

Dumare's parents actually cared. They paid attention to his likes, dislikes, nuances and they handled him well. Although Dumare's father used to sell heroin as late as the mid-seventies, he was able to be changed. While serving a five-year prison sentence Curtis became a member of the Nation of Gods and Earths. A group started by Clarence 13x Smith in seventies who had separated himself from the Nation of Islam over differences in the teachings of Elijah Muhammad and Fard Muhammad. *'Knowledge of self'* had completely changed Curtis's outlook on life and instilled morals that before he had lacked. Family meant the world to him now. He always made time for his wife and children. Tonight, was no different. He was holding a cipher with his two sons, Sincere and Dumare, and his newborn daughter Asiya, who was snuggled close to her mother Makita.

Ciphers were important because they gave the family a chance to build on positivity and destroy negativity. Curtis had explained to Dumare that a cipher was simply a gathering of men and women who intended to build righteously. These gatherings were called ciphers because knowledge, wisdom and understanding created a complete circle, or, cipher. They would bring forth knowledge, express it in the form of wisdom or wise words and bring forth a better understanding amongst all within the gathering.

Curtis felt as though the original-man was symbolic to the sun and therefore the foundation of his family, or, universe; the life-giving and sustaining force around which his family revolved. This made him God. Dumare would listen in fascination as his father told him mysterious stories of Big-Headed Scientist creating white men through genetic mutations in laboratories on the Island of Penal; of sinister nurses pricking the brains of newborns with needles and how the barbarous nature of the Caucasoid made him the devil. Even more fascinating was hearing that he was God. Dumare was young however, so his attention span was short quite often. Fifteen minutes after they started building – the term used by his father for when one professed knowledge and another added to or, built upon it - he felt like he was right back in school or at church with his Grandmother who insisted on keeping the Christian faith relevant in her grandson's life.

"All you doing is messin dat boys head up with that racist foolishness," she would always say.

"You say the white man is the devil and the black man is God, well I live around nothing but black people and they some of the most devilish folks I know. Jesus said the only way to the father is through him."

Tonight, was a little different for Dumare however, his words were flowing. He wondered if it was that "Holy Ghost" his grandmother had spoken of so euphorically. Whatever it was, he had hardly thought about going outside to play, like most children his age were doing right now. That was until he heard a knock at the door and excused himself so he could answer it. When he opened the door Wally was standing there smiling.

"Yo, come outside for a minute, I found something on the way over here I want to show you."

Dumare was curious. Wally was always up to something and for some reason; Dumare's curiosity was never disappointed when it came to his best friend.

"What is it?"

"You know I can't show you right here dummy, ya dad would mess us up. Just come outside."

"I don't know if he'll let me." Dumare said as he motioned over his shoulder with his head.

Wally could hear Mr. Curtis telling his oldest son Sincere that,

"The world is projected outward from within, there's nothing that does not originate in consciousness itself. Consciousness is the first cause, it is the creator, it is God."

Wally shook his head and with a sarcastic look on his face said,

"Oh, he's talking about that 'stuff' again?"

Wally really liked Mr. Curtis, he thought he was the coolest guy on the planet, but he was into some really deep teachings and he used a lot of big words. When he spoke like that, he would confuse Wally a little. Dumare had told Wally that he talked like that because he was a Five Percenter but that didn't mean much to Wally. He still didn't know what a Five Percenter was.

"He might let you, just ask." Wally said.

"Look, I got this..." He pulled up his shirt and showed Dumare the dull butt of an old, black and rust, Smith & Wesson Model 15 revolver. Dumare's eyes darted back to his dad to make sure he hadn't seen the gun.

"It got bullets in it too." Wally said, adding to Dumare's intrigue.

"We gotta go get Rosco then we can test it out." Wally added, as a sparkle of mischievousness glittered, in his eyes. Eventually Mr. Curtis let Dumare go out and they were off into the streets to run wild. Dumare's lessons would once again be trumped by the lessons experience teach.

"Mom, I don't want to, please don't make me do it." Serenity cried, pleading to her mom. Darlene heard her daughter's cries, but her need for a blast was speaking decibels louder.

Darlene was over-weight, toothless, and dirty. Not even the low-life, cheap, crack addict tricks she once attracted wanted to have sex with her. Not only was she the epitome of filth but it was rumored that she had full-blown AIDS. The rumor, like most rumors, had some truth to it. Darlene was infected with H.I.V. So, though deep down inside she did regret it, all she had to offer was her eleven-year-old daughter. And now, for a twenty-dollar rock, that's exactly what she was offering, no matter how wrong, immoral, and shameful it may have been.

"Now go on girl, it ain't gon hurt you none. It'll all be over before you know it; he's faster than any man I ever known anyway."

And that, to Darlene, was supposed to comfort this scared little girl. Serenity; so young, so timorous, so broken; walked timidly over to the small two-door Chevette. Leonard, a fat greasy, shameless, drunk, licked his fat, disgusting lips as Serenity approached his car. He reached down and rubbed his erection, moaning like an animal as he thought about the trim he was about to get from this pretty, young thing. He could care less just how young she was.

"If she old enough to pee, she old enough for me." He always said jokingly to bar mates. The sad part was, this wasn't a joke in his perverted mind, he actually meant it.

Serenity got in the passenger seat. The car was steaming hot.

"Uhh, sorry baby girl, I know it's a little uncomfortable in here, the air conditioner's broke." Leonard said, eying his young, tender prey lustfully. He went to touch her face, to wipe away her tears but she turned away. Serenity looked up at her mom, her eyes, begging, pleading with her not to make her do this.

"Can't you see that I'm hurting?" Her mind said, but all Darlene kept whispering was,

"You'll be okay; he's quick, just do it and get it over with."

Leonard started the engine and pulled off and into a nearby alley. He parked and as if he could wait no longer, he unbuttoned and unzipped his jeans...

When it was all over Serenity pressed herself into the corner, tears ran down her cheeks but her face revealed the immense anger and hate she felt, towards Leonard but more so towards her mother for making her do it. She felt so much shame as she walked back into the filthy crack-house she called home. All the filthy crack addicts that had walked in and out of the house whenever they wanted to, always put their hands on her where they shouldn't of, feeling her up. She hated it, but that was nothing compared to this. She ran straight past Darlene to the bathroom where she began throwing up, cold undigested hot dogs from earlier mixed with Leonard's filth.

While she washed her mouth out in the sink, she looked at herself and more tears began to accumulate in the back of her eyes. Darlene was kicking on the door, not to see if her daughter was alright, but to get her money from her.

"Open this god damn door right now and give me my money!" She yelled. No comfort, no consoling, only an order to give her the money Serenity had just made. Serenity just sat there on the floor for a minute staring dismally at the crowd of roaches beneath the sink.

"The roach motels don't do anything, neither does the raid, they just have too many babies..."

As she thought this, she could barely hear her mother at the door. Serenity thought about all the shame, hurt, and embarrassment and disgust that she had just endured for twenty dollars; twenty dollars she doubted would ever amount to the regret she would feel for the rest of her life; twenty dollars she knew would never buy her dignity back; twenty dollars that wasn't even hers to keep. Serenity slid the two ten-dollar bills under the door and sat in the bathroom alone for hours, hugging her legs close to her chest with her head buried in her knees, a small pond of salty tears forming below her.

Flames grew rapidly, wrapping themselves around the old apartment building like big flaming arms, hugging the entire tenement as wood crackled, splintered, and fell to the ground in charcoal black lumps. The loud sound of sirens from fire trucks approaching made all the spectators cover their ears. Some babies cried loudly, afraid of the blaring sound of approaching fire engines. Neighbors from as far as two and three blocks away had come out to watch as the building burned to pieces. Rosco and his mother Juanita watched sadly as everything they owned and cherished burned to the ground, including Rosco's three-year-old little brother Petey.

Petey had been sleeping on the third floor and by the time he heard Rosco screaming...

"FIRE!"

…and smelled the smoke it was too late. He was trapped in his bedroom with nowhere to run. A wall of fire had consumed his door and was blocking him from running out of the room. He ran to the window, cryi. ng in fear. He looked outside but was too afraid to jump; it was too high. Instead, he sat in the corner of his room clutching his favorite He-Man action figure close to his chest as flames began to engulf his little body. He screamed from the fear but his soul ascended before the pain set in. The raging fire continued to cremate him as his breath left his body.

Rosco, only six at the time, was crying his eyes out and his mother Juanita, who was also crying, was furious with him. It was his fault their house had burned to the ground, she always told him about playing with fire. It was his fault her baby was dead, all his fault, and she spared no emotion when blaming him, scolding him, and filling him with guilt for what he had done.

"You killed him, you killed him."

That was all Rosco could hear in his sleep. He had developed several sleeping conditions due to the amount of stress and depression on his young mind. Some of these disorders included bruxism, insomnia, somniloquy, and obstructive sleep apnea. When he was able to sleep Rosco's dreams were very vivid and disturbing. When he was awake, it was the same thing; disturbing and haunting visions.

Rosco had been severely devastated by the death of his little brother and began, with the help of his mother, to blame himself. He even attempted suicide. After months in the hospital where he was getting physical and psychological care, he was returned to his mother. The physical scars had healed but the guilt remained. On top of that, he had been returned to a home that was anything but caring, warm, or understanding. His mother did absolutely nothing to relieve his feelings of guilt and shame; rather, she perpetuated them by continuously reminding him of how he killed his brother. She continued telling him that she wished he would've died in that fire instead of Petey or when he had tried to kill himself.

"You deserved to."

There was no empathy in her whatsoever, and she never hesitated to remind Rosco that Petey was always her favorite son, his dad was better than Rosco's; he was a mistake to begin with.

"Any boy that would murder my son ain't no son of mine."

Roscoe became more introverted, quiet, and anti-social and the verbal abuse from his mother just didn't stop, finally his aunt stepped in and took him with her. Juanita didn't put up the slightest fight. Not only was he becoming an irritant to her but his eremitic behavior was as well.

For Rosco, moving with his aunt didn't make things any better. She was addicted to Percocet and cheap wine. She popped pain pills, drank Wild Irish Rose, and slept most of the time. At 7 years old the neglect Rosco was receiving caused him to start acting out negatively. In school he was hyper, a cut up, and the class clown. He became so misunderstood that they placed him on Ritalin, and placed him in a special class, after a child psychiatrist diagnosed him with dyslexia and attention deficit hyperactivity disorder.

All of the diagnoses were destroying Rosco psychologically. He began to feel as if he was the head case the doctors were making him out to be. The medications and special class placement led him to believe he really was hopeless. His head wasn't the problem however, it was his heart. He wished the shrinks could see. They were examining his mind when all along he was just suffering from a broken heart.

He never knew his father. His mother disowned him, he felt guilty for killing his younger brother, and his aunt was addicted to prescription medicine. She was always much too sedated to pay him any mind when they were at home together. Now he was constantly fighting, stealing and already smoking marijuana with Wally and Dumare. He seemed to be a lost cause from the start.

I

Helmand, Afghanistan 1975

The year of recovery. The U.S. is still recovering from its separation from gold in '71, and both the U.S. and Europe are experiencing a severe recession caused by the huge oil price hike in 1973. Nixon resigned from office the year before because of the "Watergate" scandal while the ex-Attorney General and two ex-presidential advisers were found guilty of Watergate cover-up charges. Russians are invading Afghanistan; the largest producer of heroin in the world - while Stevie Wonder works on music for his upcoming release "Songs in the Key of Life." And while oblivious to the world of politics and the true dynamics of the poverty in which he lives, Hamid is just trying to survive, a most difficult task considering the obstacles.

Hamid wipes the beads of sweat from his brow with the backs of his hands as he lances the plump pods of the poppy plants. Harvest time has come early this year. The crowns of the poppies have pointed up much sooner than normal this season, but the pointing up of the crowns is a signal that they are ready. It's late afternoon and some of the farmers are already scoring the capsules, letting the white gum seep out. After the gum has dried into a black tar, they'll scrape it off with wide knives.

It's over one hundred degrees in Afghanistan and the sun is at its zenith, shining brightly in the sky. Hamid - only eight years old - is working backwards through the fields, careful not to disturb the crops. The adult farmers will be back in the morning to collect the tar from the plants. Hamid stops to take a breath. He points his head toward the sky hoping to inhale some refreshing air but all he smells is the aftermath of the last opium war mixed with the recent ash and scattered debris left by the American shells that were dropped a day earlier. The stench of third world poverty lingers and the smell of perspiration rising like vapors from the sweat-soaked bodies of the poppy field workers stings the nostrils; the heat is only intensifying the smell.

Today alone three people have suffered heat strokes, one woman died from dehydration, and one man was hospitalized after a fight with another worker over water. Another ten men died two weeks ago - three American soldiers and seven Afghans - when U.S. troops were sent to uproot opium fields in the Uruzqan Province. Being as though opium is the main source of money for the country and the cornerstone of wealth and power for the drug lords that run it, President Akbar Muhammad, fears that the killings could be the opening shots of yet another opium war.

For Hamid, who's family is poor like most families in his section of Helmand, this is an everyday thing. He has learned to live around the routine sound of machine gun fire and occasional bomb dropping; to elude the dead bodies he's liable to pass every day on his way to school, and to engage in the struggle for food. His country is a war zone and has been for some time now.

At the age of three he was forced to watch as his father was executed by a firing squad. The AK 47 bullet left blood pouring from his eyes, nose and mouth. It was Hamid's first encounter with death but most certainly not his last.

Like most impoverished children all Hamid had was hope and dreams. At eight he was the brother of three sisters and his mom's only son, and already he had taken over the role of his father as man of the house. Working for crumbs and striving diligently to restore his family's pride and faith in Allah.

Finally, Hamid's shift was over and he and his friend Luqman made their daily three-mile journey on foot back to their homes in Helmand.

"I really wish I had enough money to leave this place for good." Luqman said. His ideas were always full of grandeur. He was the more antsy, overanxious, and naive of the two, while Hamid on the other hand was calm, reserved, calculating, and wise beyond his years. He was much more in tune with reality.

"Insha'Allah someday my friend," Hamid said.

"Insha'Allah someday we will be rich, and we will move our families out of this hell, Inshallah ta'ala." Luqman replied

"Surely Allah sees all that we do and will bless us for remaining faithful." Hamid said calmly before making a silent supplication in his heart.

"He will Hamid, I know it! We will buy big palaces, bigger than the one Shah Jahan built for his wife Arjumard Banu Begum in India and we will have servants of our own."

"The Taj Mahal?" Hamid asked.

"Yes!" Luqman answered.

Hamid knew this was all wishful thinking. There was a class system in his country where the rich got richer and the poor usually died poor. Still, he believed with hard work and dedication, he could break the cycle and at least gain a comfortable lifestyle.

"Luqman, what would you do to get rich?" Hamid asked seriously. Luqman, being his normal exuberant self said,

"Anything! I hate being poor, I hate the way people look down on me and my family. What about you?"

Hamid just smiled,

"Well, the Prophet Muhammad, peace and blessings of Allah be upon him said, 'Riches are not from abundance of worldly goods, but from a contented mind.' The prophet also said, 'Look to those inferior to yourselves, so that you may not hold Allah's benefits in contempt.'"

"Yes, but what can a man expect to accomplish without money, we are poor Hamid, who is inferior to us?"

"As Muslims, we must accept the Qadar or the divine preordainments of Allah. Whatever he wills, good or bad, we must accept. A thing that seems good to us may be bad for us and a thing that seems bad to us may be good for us. Allah subhanahu wa ta'ala says in Al-Qur'an, 'To Him belong the keys of the heavens and the earth. He enlarges provision for whom he wills, and straitens it for whom he wills. Verily, he is the All-Knower of everything.'"

"But there are men with much wealth and many children...Even some Muslim men."

"Allah ta'ala says, 'Wealth and sons are allurements of the life of this world; but the things that endure, good deeds, are best in the sight of your Lord, as rewards, and best as the foundation for hopes'...But don't worry Luqman, I feel the same as you do my friend. We must stop at the market on our way home; I have to get milk and eggs for Umi." Hamid told Luqman, whose head was still in the clouds.

As they walked through the packed market, Luqman stopped to tie his sandals, Hamid continued on at a slow pace. As Luqman stood up and ran to catch up with his friend, he bumped into a man wearing a black suit, black shoes, and a white shirt. Dust from Luqman stopping himself so abruptly flew up onto the man's expensive shoes and pants. Hamid turned around in time to see the man grab Luqman up by the shirt, pulling him so close that their noses were touching. Luqman's eyes were wide with fear as the man said,

"You really should watch where you're going; you may run into the wrong person."

The threat was noted by Luqman.

Hamid ran up beside the man.

"Please sir, he's not very cautious, sometimes he moves too fast. He sometimes acts before he thinks; I promise you he meant no disrespect. I'll get a rag and wipe your shoes, please just let him go."

The man let Luqman's shirt go and stared at Hamid.

"You resemble someone, who is your father?"

Grief washed over Hamid's face.

"He's dead sir. His name was Hamid Abdual El-Qasar."

The man pondered the name for a minute, his index and middle fingers pressed against his temple, his bodyguards looking at him curiously, wondering what he was thinking. The man began to smile. Of course, he knew who Hamid's' father was. He too was a former Drug lord who at one time controlled sixty percent of all the opium being grown in Afghanistan. He had foolishly tried to get into politics but once his background had been checked it was discovered that besides, morphine and codeine, he had been using the opium extracted from his plants to make heroin, which he sold on the black market. He was executed in front of his family and all of his homes, fields, cars, and belongings were confiscated, forcing his family into a life of poverty.

This had all happened while Nasser was still climbing the ladder; before he reached the position, he was now comfortably in. It was actually Hamid El-Qasar's passing that allowed him to reach the heights of power he had. Before his death, Hamid controlled the underworld as well as the mainstream sell of the opium extracted from his plants, which was used to make pharmaceutical drugs. He had to be worth well over 3 billion dollars before his execution, minus his liquidable assets.

Nasser looked at the boy who couldn't have been any older than two or three when El-Qasar was murdered.

"He probably has no idea of the opulent life he would have inherited had it not been for his father's big-headedness," he thought,

"The boy probably thinks he was born poor." He said to himself before finally breaking the long uncomfortable silence his reverie had caused.

"Your father was a great man." He said to Hamid, who was just happy that the man was no longer angry.

"My name is Nasser, Nasser Saladin." He said extending his hand to Hamid, who shook it hesitantly.

"And what is your name my little friend?" Nasser asked looking back to Luqman. Luqman told him his name reluctantly, he was still nervous.

"Well Luqman, I'm sorry for scaring you but you really should be more careful, there are men out here whose tempers are much shorter than mine." Nasser warned him, before refocusing his attention on Hamid.

"I understand your family is very poor now."

It was more of a statement than a question.

"Yes, we are very poor sir. I am here to get eggs and milk and I have not enough money to pay for that even. I must ask the lady there in the blue hijab if she will allow me to pay next week when I receive my wages." Shame and embarrassment made Hamid's handsome face seem pitiful.

"Don't worry about asking for credit, this should cover the expenses." Nasser pulled out a stack of Afghans that was equal to five thousand American dollars. Hamid was so shocked he didn't know whether to take it or not.

"And there is whole lot more where that came from. I'm sure you will share it with your friend who I take is in the same position as you as far as food and money is concerned."

"Of course," Hamid said, and he split the money in half right in front of Nasser.

"I want you to meet my friend Tariq here at dusk. For now, on you will be working for me." Nasser began thinking of Hamid's mother. She should be no older than 28 now. Hamid El-Qasar had married her when she was 18. She was probably still just as beautiful as she had been as El-Qasar's bride; Nasser wanted her for himself now.

"Also be sure to tell your mother that I would like to meet with her so she should accompany you tonight."

"What about my sisters? There are three of them." Hamid asked.

"Bring them too. Oh, and your friend Luqman, bring him also, as I can see he is your closest companion."

Nasser excused himself and the boys let out the big smiles they had been holding in since Nasser handed them the money.

"Look at all this money Hamid, Masha 'Allah! Allah willed it! Oh you were right, Allah is truly benevolent and beneficent, Ar-rahman, Ar-rahim."

Hamid said, "Alhamdu lillahi. Yes, he is Luqman."

"My mother will be so pleased." Luqman continued. He didn't stop until they reached their town and parted ways.

"He said dusk." Hamid reminded Luqman.

"We should leave right after Maghrib prayer. It is a three mile walk to the market so we must be sure to leave early."

"OK." Luqman said, and they each headed home.

II

"Where did you get this money from?"
Luqman's mother asked. She was very pious, very
God-fearing.

"A man gave it to me at the market. His name
was Nasser, Nasser Sal..." Before he could get the
rest of the name out, his mother's hand came down
on his face with a loud smack. He could taste the
blood in his mouth and he stuck his tongue into the
cut on the inside of his cheek.

"You are to give that money back! It is haram
money and that man is evil. It is he who keeps us
poor."

Luqman thought his mother was blinded by
her own hate; he had just given them twenty-five-
hundred dollars; how was he keeping them poor? No,
it was she who was now keeping them poor.

"But Umi, we need the money." Luqman
reasoned.

"Silence! You will give the money back and
I don't want any more back-talk, do you understand?"
Her eyes were intense, angry, and he knew he'd better
just keep quiet while he was ahead.

"Yes Umm."

The scene at Hamid's house was much different than the one at Luqman's. Maleeka, Hamid's mother, smiled brightly when she saw the money.

"Where did you get all this money?" She asked surprised. Hamid smiled, happy just to bring his mother and sisters some joy. They all spent most of their days so miserable.

"Nasser Saladin, and he wants to meet with you mama."

Maleeka blushed. She knew very well who Nasser Saladin was and she was shocked to hear that he wanted to meet with her. She hadn't been with a man since her husband passed.

"I don't know Hamid; I don't have very many pretty things left. The government took most of my garbs and jewelry."

"I don't think he cares mama, he seemed to like you a lot. He knew papa too."

Maleeka was absolutely incredible physically. Her skin was the color of polished bronze. Her hair was long, the texture of smooth silk, jet black and ran down to the small of her back. She never wore makeup; she didn't need to. Her Persian features were impeccable; high cheek bones, nice pouting lips, a slender up-turned nose, and dark gorgeous eyes. She was a princess in every sense of the word, albeit, a poor one.

"What about your sisters?" Maleeka asked.

"He said you can bring them too."

Maleeka had experienced good living so living without it was like torture. She knew Nasser was her only chance to get her former life back. He was wealthy, very wealthy, maybe even more than her widower. Through Nasser and his organization, Afghanistan was the world's top heroin producer, supplying between 35% and 90% of the global market. He was a strong man with power and most importantly, connections. He single-handedly battled President Akbar Muhammad's government without the help of any neighboring countries, only fellow drug lords. This of course was the reason for the violent civil war that was now taking place in the country. This power and importance only attracted Maleeka to him even more.

"Was your mother happy, when you gave her the money?" Hamid asked Luqman as he, and his family made the journey back to the town the market was held in.

"No, she told me to give it back to Mr. Saladin. She said it was Shaitans' money…Haram money…"

Luqman sounded disappointed.

"I'm sorry my friend but we cannot fault our parents for trying to protect us from evil. You should not even be upset with her. Allah says 'The Lord hath decreed that ye be dutiful to your parents, and say not to them a word of contempt, address them in terms of honor, lower to them the wings of humility and say My Lord, bestow on them thy mercy as they cherished me in childhood."

After losing his father, Hamid began reading the Qur'an his father had given him. It had helped him get through very difficult times and now that he was logging the Surahs and Ayahs to memory, they were becoming a guide for his young life.

"I'm not giving it back though," Luqman said defiantly.

"I wouldn't expect you to my friend. Astagfurllah, pray for forgiveness for disobeying your Umm." Hamid said, smiling at his friend.

"I wonder what kind of job Mr. Saladin has for us." Luqman said curiously. He would soon find out that the plan Nasser had for him and Hamid was nothing like what he had in mind.

As the limousine that had picked them up from the market place approached Nasser's palace, Hamid stared at the gold minaret that rose from the top of the Mansions' roof. Maleeka too was in a daydream. Remembering when Hamid's father once had such wealth. She was young, a runaway orphan from Persia. He had quickly married her before anyone else could. And she bore him four kids in six years. Now watching as this architectural gem grew bigger the closer they got, she knew she had to perform well to enjoy that life style once again.

Nasser stood in the doorway, below the portico with its ivory columns and Corinthian capitals. He wore a satin robe and his right hand held a glass of red wine, Domaine du Mas Blanc Collioure. His bright white smile was wide as

Maleeka stepped out of the limousine. The kids walked in first. Nasser kissed the hands of all three Hamid's sisters, than shook the hands of Luqman and Hamid

"My little friends...thank you for accepting my invitation."

He then leaned down and whispered,

"Were your families happy with the money?"

Hamid said,

"My mother was happy; we really needed it, thank you."

Luqman, a little slower to speak said,

"My mother was angry with me, she slapped my face and told me I was to return the money to you, I saved it though, she was speaking out of anger."

"Ahh, smart boy," Nasser said as he led them in the house.

"I like you two. Night and Day...but you complement each other."

Maleeka, stepping slowly, measuredly, and gracefully towards Nasser, bowed once she was close to him. He took her soft hand in his. She pulled away before his lips could touch her skin. Nasser understood, she was striving hard to be a pious Muslimah.

"I'm glad you came." he whispered into her ear. The words and the brush of his warm breath against her flesh sent a chill through her body. She had nearly forgotten the effect a charming man could have on her. Nasser led her inside and his body guards sealed the door behind them.

Immediately the ambrosial aroma of frankincense, myrrh, and jessamine filled Maleeka's nose with a delightful sensation. This debauchery had all of her senses tingling. Nasser offered her a glass of wine but she refused

"I don't drink." She said respectfully.

"Alhamdu lillahi." Nasser said.

"Allahumaghfirli warhamni...O Allah forgive me and have mercy on me." He added, knowing he too was sinning by consuming alcohol. For Nasser however, the fact that he dealt in the illicit trade of drugs and usury, both haram in Islam, it was easy for other forms of sin to creep into his life. Nasser made another du'a silently then gave Maleeka a tour of his estate.

It was luxurious. Rugs from China and Persia, paintings from Paris, it perfectly meshed the gracious ambiance of Asia's antiquitous past with its modernizing future. There was expansive living and dining room space, a library that was almost the size of Maleeka's entire house, a large media room. It was like a dream to the kids.

Maleeka and Nasser shared small talk while they climbed the grand circular staircase that led to the second floor where his master bedroom was. The children were all amazed. The place was more a museum than a home to them. Nasser led them outside onto one of the hugs roof terraces, which like the large arched windows, supplied breathtaking, panoramic views of Afghanistan and its now star-lit skyline. Maleeka was floored.

"He is even wealthier than Hamid." she thought as she contemplated all she had been shown.

That night as the kids slept comfortably, Nasser was forced to restrain himself. Maleeka was religious and he respected that.

"I was thinking we should send the kids to America for schooling." Nasser said.

He made it sound as if he was looking out for the kids' interest but his real motive was to set them up in America so they could be groomed by his legion of rebels already stationed in the United States.

"I don't know; my children are my life." Maleeka said seriously. She wasn't too fond of the idea of sending them away like that.

"I understand that Maleeka but look at this country, it's a war zone. The people are fighting among themselves as well as with the U.S. Troops. With the amount of bloodshed there's no guarantee your children will even live until tomorrow."

"But I figured you asking me here tonight was an invitation to come and live with you, and you have your own army, can't you protect us?"

"You figured right. I do want you to live with me; I want you to be my wife. I also want what is best for your children, which is, sending them to America to be schooled without the interruption of bombings and machine gun fire. Once they are of age they will come back and Hamid and Luqman will work for me and eventually inherit my position."

Soon Maleeka agreed and two years later, Hamid, Luqman, Halima, Fatima and Amelia were sent to America to become citizens and begin their schooling.

Hamid and Luqman, followed by Hamid's sisters, were led by one of Nasser's friends to Brooklyn after arriving in New York City. Brooklyn's Atlantic Avenue was closer in resemblance to an epicenter in the Middle East than an American street. This particular area had the densest concentration of Arabs. Hamid, Luqman and Hamid's sisters felt at home along those gritty and packed streets. There were many Muslims, in traditional Islamic dress crowded near the Islamic community centers and bookshops. Middle Eastern restaurants, grocery stores and bakeries, smoke shops, translation services, and hairdressers all seemed to be owned by Arabs and it was this fact that Luqman took the most heed to. He could not help but think he would easily become rich in America. Some men gathered in small groups at outdoor cafes, sipping minted tea and smoking from bubbling hookahs. Women in layered skirts and scarves, babies in tow, walk several paces behind the men. On Fridays, during Jumu'ah, when the mosques filled, the Muslims who could not fit in the mosque would simply throw down small prayer rugs or place newspapers on the sidewalk and prostrate themselves toward the Kaaba in Mecca.

This was the scene that welcomed Hamid and Luqman and they were overjoyed. The very first Friday they made their way to the Masjid and before prayer, listened to the religious sermon given by the Imam. It was the beginning of their schooling and lives as American Muslims and by 1986; they were well transitioned into American society.

III

Wally and Dumare walked the last two blocks to Rosco's house in a hurry. They smiled when they got to his door.

"You think it shoots?" Dumare asked. His mind was still on the gun in Wally's waist.

"It's a gun, why wouldn't it?"

After two knocks Rosco came to the door smiling brightly as always when seeing his two favorite people in the world. Wally and Dumare were the best things that ever happened to Rosco; they took his mind off of his problems. He never needed therapy or medicine, he needed friends and love.

"Wussup yall?" He asked. His lips were stained red from the popsicle he was sucking on.

"What up, can you come out?" Wally asked his younger cousin, knowing that even if he wasn't allowed to, he would anyway. Especially after Wally showed him what he had tucked behind his belt.

"Check this out." Wally said, lifting his shirt just enough for Rosco to see the gun.

"Oh snap, where you get that from?" Rosco asked, throwing his cherry Popsicle.

"Is it real?"

He inched closer so he could get a better look at the firearm. The gun was definitely old, the rust verified that. The barrel was pitted and the butt was unnaturally small. It looked like it had been through a few wars; the tape around the handle corroborated that theory.

"Yeah it's real man, now come on, we gon make sure it work."

"Alright, hold on one second." Rosco ran back in the house, grabbed his FILA wind breaker, and came running outside; the excitement in his face clearly visible now.

"Where we goin?" Dumare and Rosco asked simultaneously.

"Ummmm," Wally thought,

"We can go over to Cambridge Street, to the shed in back of Mr. Woody's house." Even in their early days it was Wally making the majority of the decisions.

"What if he's home?" Dumare asked. He was always the careful one. He had to be, he had the most to fear considering he was he the only one that had a family that actually cared for him and would punish him for misbehaving. Wally and Rosco basically had nothing to lose. It made them display fearlessness that was sometimes on the verge of carelessness while Dumare displayed caution that sometimes resembled cowardice. The trio balanced each other out.

"He ain't home, it's three o'clock, he still at work, and even if he is, we'll just find another spot."

Wally said, and with that they headed over to Cambridge.

As they walked Wally's chest was poked out a little farther than usual because of what he had now; even at ten the gun gave him a feeling of power; he felt fearless.

"And where you think you goin?" Darlene asked Serenity. Serenity hadn't spoken to her mother since the day before when she made her commit that awful act with a man that was old enough to be her grandfather. She hated her mother for it, and would for the rest of her life.

"Outside," she said angrily, not even stopping to hear what Darlene's response would be. She knew she would have something to say about her going out, she always did, but at this moment, Serenity could care less. Her plans were to leave today and never come back.

"Well, you make sure you have your butt back in this house by..."

Serenity never heard the rest; the door was already closed. She pulled the three dollars she had stolen out of her mother's drawer and walked into the mini grocery store at the end of her block. She hadn't eaten all day and she felt like her ribs were literally touching.

As she made her way through the small store her eyes fell on a pretty girl of around twenty-one or twenty-two. She had on big gold bangles and bamboo earrings. Her weave was woven tightly and she had on an enviable expensive Gucci suit. Serenity couldn't stop staring. The only time she did stop was to look down at her own pathetic rags and make a comparison...there was none. She made a mental note to get an outfit just like that one.

After Serenity paid for her food, she walked outside. The same girl was standing beside the pay phone. There was a lot of admiration for the girl from Serenity, who liked the way the girl dressed, the way she walked, the way all the boys were looking at her. Serenity built up the nerve to talk to her.

"Excuse me," she said nervously. The girl rolled her eyes at Serenity as if her mere existence irritated her.

"I like your outfit." Serenity said innocently. The girl let out a faint smile this time. No matter how pompous, a stroke to the ego was never irritating.

"Well thank you." She said still shunning Serenity.

"I wish I could get something like that." Serenity continued to press the issue, and also hoping to maybe make a friend. She knew she had a many lonely nights ahead of her; it would help to have somebody she could hang out it with.

"You can sweetie, you see this?" The girl said placing her hands on her hips, accentuating her derrière.

"You can get whatever you want with this honey, trust me."

Serenity just smiled. She didn't quite get what the girl was saying but she had an idea. She was about to say something else when a car pulled up in front of them and beeped.

"Oh, sorry honey. I gotta go, this..." she pointed at her back side again, " is about to get me these Dior shoes I been dying to get. Just remember what I said, anything you want..."

Serenity just stood there for a minute, pondering whatever wisdom the Girl in the Gucci Suit had tried to impart

Leonard had given her twenty dollars just to...

Serenity decided not to remind herself. She walked away from the store, not really knowing where she was going, but absolutely sure it wasn't back to that crack and whore house she used to call home. She turned the corner onto Cambridge Street and smiled when she saw Wally, Dumare and Rosco. They all knew each other from school, but the smile was mostly because of the crush she had on Wally. The boys saw Serenity as soon as she saw them but didn't look as happy about it as she did. Wally had been waiting for almost a half an hour now to shoot his gun and now here was something else to slow him down.

"Hey Wally, where y'all goin?" Serenity asked once they were closer. The boys all looked at each other and silently it was agreed upon, it was up to Wally to make the call.

"Nowhere, we just..."

Rosco cut in.

"We got a gun and we bout to go to old man Woody's shed to shoot it."

He just couldn't control himself.

"No, we're not." Dumare said, while Wally smacked the back of Rosco's head.

"Shut up stupid!" Wally said, angered by Rosco's talkative nature.

"I knew we shouldn't have brought him, he too young anyway." Dumare said angrily.

"Oooh, I want to come." Serenity said.

"No. No girls allowed." Wally said.

"Why not?" Serenity asked defensively.

"Because I said so, that's why." Wally's voice was growing gradually louder the more upset he got.

"Well I'm tellin then." Serenity said rolling her eyes. Wally sucked his teeth. He hated being beat by a girl, at anything.

"Alright, you can come, but you better not say nothing and you aint shootin it." Wally said

"Why not?" She asked again just being difficult, she was young but already felt like she was being discriminated against by the boys just for being a girl.

"Cause girls don't shoot guns." Rosco interjected.

"Who said?"

"Everybody knows that." Rosco added.

"You too young to know anything." Serenity shot back at him.

"Am not!"

"Are so!"

"Shut up y'all, damn, just come on. Serenity you're not shootin the gun!" Wally snapped, this time nobody argued.

IV

The shed was right behind an old man named Woody's house and the back of the shed had two windows that faced the alleyway behind it. The dust inside of the old hand-built shack was thick. Serenity sneezed.

"Shhhhhh." Wally said with his finger to his lips.

"Sorry." She apologized, covering her mouth.

It was dark, filled with wood and old car parts. It smelled like a musty basement, and all four of them covered their noses with their shirts.

"It stinks in here Wally" Rosco complained.

"Well leave if you don't like it." Wally told Rosco who was really starting to work his nerves.

"Hey D; move that wood away from that window." Wally said.

As soon as Dumare moved the wood a ray of light illuminated a portion of the shed. They could actually see how thick the dense cloud of dust was.

"Open it too." Wally said. Once the window was open the breeze began to break apart the cloud of dust and debris. They all sat down on make-shift chairs; cans, buckets, piles of wood and anything else they could get their hands on. Serenity didn't really like the fact that the light was in the shed, now Wally

46

would be able to see her gawking at him. She still made sure her seat was right beside his.

Wally pulled out the revolver and Serenity jumped.

"You scared?" He asked, hoping she would say yeah, he liked Serenity but he wasn't too fond of having her around right now. This was boy stuff in his mind.

"No." She lied.

"Let me go first Wally, let me go first." Rosco asked excitedly.

"Man, no way! It's my gun! I'm shootin it first!" And that was that, everyone else knew not to even ask until Wally shot the gun first.

"Here you can light this first though." Wally said. He smiled at Rosco as he passed him the joint he had in his pocket since that morning.

"This is even better." Rosco said giggling. He took the matches from Wally, struck two, and lit the tip of the joint. It glowed like a bright reddish-orange tailed firefly in the dim light of the shed. The aroma didn't take long to permeate the entire area. Serenity covered her nose; she always hated the smell of joints.

Wally stood up, aimed the gun at the window, there was a loud pop... the crashing sound of shattered glass... and then... a gasp... the gasp of a man, a man trying to catch his quickly fleeing breath. Wally, still holding the warm gun in his hands, still in his imitation cop pose, was trying to catch his own

breath. His eyes were wide with fear as he hoped that
what he heard wasn't what he was thinking…
It couldn't be…
No way...

Rosco, joint still in hand, stood still with his
mouth opened wide. Dumare shared a similar look.
They both stared up at Wally in shocked terror. As
always, they were waiting for him to make a move,
or call a shot. Serenity was the only one to make a
move. She ran to the door and around to the alley.
Her inhale was deep and loud enough for the boys to
hear it back inside. It broke them out of their trances
and they ran around to the alley expecting the worst.

The three of them stood beside Serenity. On
the ground lay a skinny brown-skinned man. He was
a drug addict that Wally knew and he was bleeding
badly from the neck. A puddle of thick, dark red,
almost purple looking blood was forming around his
head. His opened eyes were glazed, opaque, and
unmoving.

"You think he still alive?" Rosco asked.

"No…he's dead…look at him…" Dumare
told him. They were all looking at the man as if he
were a science project and not someone's dead son,
or maybe even dead father.

"Well why is he still lookin at us?" Rosco
asked, this time directing his question to Wally, not
caring how he looked or sounded. This was the first
time he had actually seen death up close and personal

like this, he was intrigued. He wondered if Petey had died with his eyes still open.

"That's just how some people die." Wally told him.

"Everything just stops and if your eyes are still open, then that's just how you die."

Wally had too much on his mind now to be answering anymore of Rosco's questions.

"What are we gonna do?" Serenity asked, finally speaking again.

"We gotta go before somebody see us. Nobody better say nothin!" Wally warned them all.

As they ran away from the body, Wally just couldn't shake the startling fact that he had just killed someone.

V

"I think you should throw it away." Serenity said as she stood with Wally, Rosco, and Dumare in that alley in Wally's shabby neighborhood filled with its depressing tenements. Wally was still debating on whether or not he should get rid of the gun that had just taken a man's life. He didn't know when or how he would be able to get his hands on another one. But he was smart enough to know that if he kept it and the cops caught him with it he would be going to jail for a real long time.

"Yeah man you gotta throw it away." Dumare told him. Wally usually trusted Dumare's decisions because Dumare's pessimism and tepidness often kept them out of trouble. Wally used to call him scared but he was slowly learning that sometimes, being scared is being smart.

"I'll keep it." Rosco said. This time nobody said a word to Rosco, they all just stared at him, and the looks on their faces said enough. He shut up.

After a little more deliberation Wally wiped his prints off the gun with his shirt tail and buried it in the trash can behind a house nearby. The four of them continued on their way.

They all walked around doing much of nothing that evening and before they knew it the sun was going down and Dumare and Rosco both had to get home. Wally dreaded going home and Serenity felt as though she no longer had a home.

They all had different situations but it was one ligature that connected the four of them, one similarity that made their predicaments four different parts of the same problem. They were all feeling the effects of the crack epidemic in some form or fashion. They were all crack babies in essence, maybe not in the literal sense, but the sense that, that was the generation that was raising them.

Inevitably they were all suffering from the ubiquitous plight caused by the pestilence of rocked cocaine in America's ghettos. A Pestilence that was causing hundreds of thousands of infants to be born each year, addicted and physically deformed with cocaine induced damage. It was a pestilence that was causing some mothers to abandon their children on doorsteps and in decrepit alleys; a pestilence that was causing mothers to not care about anyone or anything but that next blast.

VI

That night, Wally tried to sleep through the hunger pangs in his growling stomach and the nauseating smell of crack being burned that filled the decrepit apartment. He tossed and turned, covered his face in the pillow, and wiped away tears. He was hurting internally though he never let it show in public. His young heart was soar; his once optimistic youthful eyes had lost their innocent glimmer three years ago when the sound of gunshots woke him up out of his sleep. He had walked down the stairs to see his father laid out flat in the center of the living room, a circle of dark blood still growing bigger and bigger around his body, his mom crying, looking up at him as if to say do something but realizing there was nothing he could do. He had felt hopeless at that moment.

Now he was either angry or confused most of the time, his only happiness was his friends. After the death of his dad, the doctors had diagnosed him with Post-Traumatic Stress disorder, saying the image of his dead father surrounded by the blood, the noise, the crying, all of it had scarred his young mind and he would now experience episodes of stress, depression, and anxiety attacks for a while but that there was a chance he could grow out of it. Tonight, he was really depressed but again refused to take the medication that had been prescribed for him. He lay awake in his bed listening to the loud thunder, watching the silver rain fall outside, the wind splashing rain drops against his window, he thought about his father, and hated when thoughts of his mother surfaced. The mixture was too depressing.

Across town, Dumare sat in his room in the same position, staring at the rain and the bright metallic-blue flashes of lightening. His heart was soar also but it wasn't something at home; he hurt for Wally. He felt bad for Rosco and Serenity too, but mostly for Wally. They had been best friends since they could talk and he hated what Wally had to live through. They were like two organs in the same body, he was the brain, Wally was the heart, and whenever the heart was broken the brain knew.

His father had once told him that the son of man causes rain, hail, sleet, and snow...if only he could stop the storms in his comrades' soul. He wondered why God allowed Wally to experience such pain. His grandmother always told him to just have faith in Jesus because God worked in mysterious ways while his father was telling him he was God. That night his reason led him to question why he felt so powerless if he was God and why his Grandmother's God didn't just ease all of the suffering they were facing.

Not too far away from Wally's house, Serenity was drenched in the rain, but was determined to never, ever, go back home. She huddled like a ball in the doorway of someone's house and watched the tiny rain drops splash the tips of her worn down Pro-Keds sneakers. She was shivering from the cold, and she was in a tug a war with her tiny jacket with the wind.

Serenity's household had never been filled with the spirit of God. Her mother's only religion was drugs. Still, somewhere along the way she had been introduced to the concept. On this particular night, she knew she needed something higher than herself to get her through this. Serenity clasped her wet hands and bowed her head.

"God, I don't know if you're out there, but I would really like for you to help me...well, not just me, but Wally and Rosco and Dumare too. I know we did something really bad today but I hope you can forgive us...we're sorry. God, please give me a place to stay. I promise to be good if you do...A'..."

Before she could say Amen, a man's voice interrupted her.

"Hey pretty girl, why are you sitting out here in the rain? Haven't you got anywhere to go?" He asked, trying to comfort this forlorn girl.

Serenity looked away from the man and into the empty streets. The rain was coming down hard now and the scenery looked blurry. She looked back at the old man. His face was definitely seasoned. He had a soaked, black skull cap on his head and an outfit that looked like it was most likely a handout from the Goodwill or Salvation Army. His pinkish wrinkled hands gripped a bottle of strong liquor, 151, but it wasn't really his appearance that Serenity was paying attention to, it was the bad vibes she was getting from him.

He seemed nice enough, but he scared her. Something was wrong with this man she thought as a Corona of negative energy shown around him. Her intuition was telling her something. The vibe was so strong his shadiness seemed visible; it was like watching the dark, ominous clouds that precede a storm just waiting for the bad to come. She was cold however, and hungry, and tired, and lonely...

"I don't have anywhere to go." She said, finally.

"Oh, well I couldn't let a cute little thing like you sleep out here in the rain, c'mon; I'll take you to my apartment. Ain't got much, few extra blankets and an extra pillow, you could sleep on the chair in the front room." The man said generously as he held his hand out for her, he looked nice enough; she took his hand and let him help her up. Serenity tried to convince herself that the bad feeling she had about the man was just her being paranoid.

"I don't have any money". She told the man.

"Well good, I wouldn't have taken it anyway sweetheart, now c'mon so we can go dry you off."

Serenity thought about it again, and then followed the man to his apartment. He wasn't lying, he sure didn't have much. The stove was already open when they came in.

"Cut my heat off last month…" He said as if it was nothing,

"Should be back on first thing next month though."

Serenity pulled up a chair and sat by the open stove.

"Well, I got some hot dogs; a couple packs of Oodles and Noodles, and some cheese for some grilled cheese sandwiches. So, what'll it be young lady, hot dogs and noodles, or grilled cheese sandwiches?"

Serenity smiled when he called her young lady. He was nice, comforting and he sounded just like her grandpa, before he had his heart-attack. The only difference was the man's race.

"Grilled cheese," she said with a smile. He noticed the smile and he liked it, it was warming, it had been a long time since he'd had a friend that wasn't a junky in his apartment, especially a lady.

"Well, I'll do you one better sweetheart, how bout we fry up those hot dogs, cut em in half and put em between the grilled cheese, I don't know about you but I ain't ate all day."

Serenity hadn't either, but by the sounds coming from her stomach, you would think she hadn't eaten in a week.

"OK." She wasn't about to turn him down. She took off her jacket and hung it on the back of her chair, she was still soaking wet.

"Oh, I'm sorry, let me take that, I'll go get you a towel and those covers, that way you can dry off and wrap up in the blanket and we'll hang up your clothes by the stove so they can dry."

The man disappeared into the back and came back with a shabby old gray wool blanket and a towel. Serenity wiped her face and hair with the towel then asked where the bathroom was so she could take her clothes off.

"Down the hall; first door on the left."

Serenity noticed a change in the man's eyes when he said this. That ominous look was back and her heart fluttered with fear. She walked to the bathroom with the towel and blanket in hand, the hallway was dark. There was no doorknob on the bathroom door, so she just pulled it closed, and hoped it wouldn't swing open.

The bathroom reeked of fresh urine on top of old, stale urine. It lined the inside of the toilet bowl and changed the white porcelain toilet seat to a dingy yellow. The tub was filthy, filled with gray grime, greenish slime near the drain and brown rust around the faucet. In the corners of the ceiling were layers upon layers of gossamer filled with flies and roaches. Serenity wrinkled her nose at the sights and smells of the gross bathroom, then sat the blanket on top of the toilet lid after wiping it off. Her shoes and socks were soaked; she kicked those off first, then the rest of her clothes until she was down to her underwear.

There was a noise out in the hallway... a floorboard creaked... somebody was coming...

slowly... Serenity was scared. A spasm of fear shot through her body... she watched the door closely... in the black hole where the doorknob used to be, an eyeball appeared... it stared at her, lustfully... blinked, then disappeared. The footsteps in the hallway were hurried this time. Finally, she exhaled as the apparent danger subsided.

Serenity thought she would cry she was so scared. She quickly wrapped herself back up in the blanket, carried her clothes in her arm and walked timidly back to the kitchen.

"Almost done." The man said cheerfully, once again smiling. Serenity stared at his eyes. They were definitely the same eyes that had watched her undress.

After they ate, they sat in front of the 13 inch, black and white TV.

"Don't get that many channels, but sometimes if you smack it up a little, you can get two or three pretty clear." The man said to Serenity who was pulling the cover extra tight around her now. Not only was she cold, but she was still slightly nervous. As they ate the man never took his eyes off of her.

At the same time, she was thankful to the man for feeding her and giving her a place to sleep, she was actually full right now, and dry. The rain outside had slowed down to a drizzle and it was one o'clock in the morning now.

"I think my clothes are dry now," Serenity said, not really caring if they were or not. She put them on in the kitchen, they were still slightly damp but she put them on anyway. When she sat back down, she looked at the old man who was finishing the last of his liquor, and wondered if it would be scarier to sleep outside or to sleep in here with this creepy old man.

VII

That night Rosco walked in the house to once again find his aunt passed out in her favorite chair. His house wasn't the best, but it wasn't the worst either. Wally and Serenity had it the worst out of the four of them…by far. In his house there was just the absence of attention. Tonight, he was alright with that however; if she were awake, she surely would have noticed that something was on his mind.

"Now me and Wally both killed somebody." he thought as he made his way to his bedroom.

Rosco stared at the same rain that Wally and Dumare were. He listened to the sound of booming thunder and the pitter-patter of the rain drops against his roof. Rosco hated the rain; it always came at the wrong times. Why couldn't it have come when Petey was burning? Now Petey was gone and so was his mother. Crack had beaten her too. The number of victims that drug had claimed in its short existence was unreal.

Juanita always told Rosco that her addiction was also his fault, that he had driven her to it and that if she still had her baby everything would have been alright. The truth of the matter was; Juanita could never accept responsibility for her own shortcomings. Rosco was the only scapegoat she had.

She was his mom so he simply believed her when she said everything was his fault. At times it got so tough for him he wished he would go to sleep at night and never wake up.

If it wasn't for Wally and Dumare, he would have taken a whole bottle of his aunts Percocet a long time ago. He was so young yet already suicidal, but so full of life when with his friends. And as the rain continued to splash against his roof it was them that he thought of.

Something felt terribly wrong tonight however. Rosco felt like somebody was hurt or about to get hurt. He just couldn't shake the feeling. It was so strong that it kept him up half the night. He watched as the pouring rain slowed to a drizzle, wondering what he was feeling.

Serenity felt a soft tug at her zipper and her eyes began to open slowly. Those eyes...they were staring at her again. Now her eyes were wide open and she could see that the man's lust had finally taken over him. He looked dangerous now, like a monster almost. His sneer was menacing and the look in his eyes was malicious. He pulled aggressively at her zipper and this time it came all the way down.

She fought back and cried, "STOP, stop it please," But he was already past the point of no return. He had been watching her sleep for almost twenty minutes. She looked so peaceful and pure, just like a little angel, and Lord knows it had been a while since he had had a woman He tugged at her pants, but she desperately held them up.

"Only if I was a little bit younger," he thought, noticing he didn't have the strength he used to.

"No, I don't want to mister; please don't make me do that." Serenity cried as she held on to the top of her jeans for dear life.

"I fed you god damn it, I was nice to you, now be nice to me." He said angrily. Serenity managed to sit up straight, and the man finally backed up. When he did Serenity stood up and took her foot to his crotch. He howled and doubled over in pain and Serenity ran out of the house.

The rain had picked up dramatically, but she barely noticed it as she ran and ran. She kept running blindly until she got to Wally's apartment. She was drenched, and now, exhausted. It was 1:30 in the morning and she knew he would probably be sleep but she had to try.

Wally heard a noise at his window. He looked at the window curiously. A rock ricocheted off the glass for a second time. He looked down and saw Serenity looking up at him, her eyes filled with sadness, her clothes drenched in rain. He jumped up and threw on his clothes and slipped on his sneakers. He always acted so tough around her, but inside he had a soft spot for Serenity.

He snuck past the zombie who was in her usual position; arm hanging off the sofa, crack-pipe nearby. When he got outside, Serenity was sitting on the steps crying.

"What's wrong?" Wally asked, wrapping his arms around her. Whatever happened, she was real shook up about it.

"This man... this old man, he tried to do it to me. I kept telling him to stop but he just wouldn't."

"You want to sleep here tonight?" Wally asked her.

Serenity looked up at him kind of surprised. He always acted like she barely existed, but now, not only was she able to confide in him, he was even trying to comfort her.

"What is your mom gonna say?" She asked wiping the mixture of rain and tears from her face.

"She ain't goin say nuttin, she sleep." Wally said before sneaking her upstairs. Once they were in his room, Wally looked around for something Serenity could sleep in.

"Here, you can put this on." Wally said handing Serenity one of his hand-me-down Champion Tees.

"And here's some shorts. Just put your clothes on the radiator so they can dry."

Serenity took off her clothes and Wally draped them over the radiator for her. Serenity put on the clothes he handed her and just stood there looking awkward, where was she supposed to sleep?

"You look like a little boy." Wally said teasing her.

"Shut up, where am I supposed to lay?"

Wally looked around the room then back at Serenity.

"You can sleep in my bed if you want, I won't mess with you." He said.

"OK," Serenity said bashfully before climbing into the bed and under the covers. They were so far apart at first that if either one of them rolled to the wrong side they would be on the floor. That was until Serenity said,

"I'm cold." Wally got the hint. He came closer and wrapped his arms around her like he had seen his dad do with his mom a long, long time ago. Soon they were both asleep, Rosco and Dumare too. None of them knowing that tomorrow would shape and mold the rest of their lives.

VIII

"Get y'all little hot selves out of this bed." The zombie screamed tugging at the sheets on Wally's bed with her bony arms.

"Who's this fresh lil girl you got up in my house?"

Serenity was scared, so that's why Wally never wanted to come home. Last night his room had seemed so warm and comforting that she didn't notice what the sunlight was now revealing. The room was ragged, and way under-furnished. There was a giant hole in the wall and nothing but a bed and a six-drawer dresser that only had three drawers. And this woman, who looked more like a skeleton than a woman. So, this is who Wally was always referring to as the "zombie", this was her first time at Wally's' house and she wasn't too thrilled about coming back.

"What you starin at?" Wally's mom asked Serenity who didn't realize she was staring so blatantly.

"Nuh, nothing," Serenity stuttered.

"Ya, little hot in the pants ass, where ya mom at?"

"Just get dressed Serenity."

Wally wasn't in the mood to argue with his mom, he never was for that matter. He viewed her as an insubstantial part of his life; a woman whose existence didn't warrant any of his attention or energy.

"Don't you be bringing none of your little girlfriends into my house Wally, I mean that!"

"Whatever." Wally whispered as he pulled his shirt down over his head.

"What you say?" The zombie asked.

Wally didn't respond, just stared at her malevolently and shook his head in disgust.

"Oh, I thought so,"

Wally grabbed Serenity's hand and they ran out the door.

When Wally knocked on Dumare's door and his best-friend saw who he was with, his eyes squinted interrogatively. He looked a little puzzled, but also amused. Serenity had never walked to school with them before, but he decided not to speak on it. He would wait until he and Wally were alone. He did want to know what Wally was up to however. He wouldn't have to wait until they were alone after all, Rosco, never one to hold his tongue asked,

"What she doin here?" as he stood in his doorway.

Serenity and Wally looked at each other and shared a smile, as they thought about last night and the zombie this morning. Dumare looked at Wally with his eyebrows raised accusingly and shook his head, he knew now.

"Don't worry about it." Wally told Rosco and they started their six-block journey to their school. As they walked Rosco remembered the funny feeling he had last night.

"I couldn't go to sleep last night." He said.

"Me either." Dumare added.

"I know, that rain kept me up late last night too, that and this feeling..." Wally didn't finish because the thought of Serenity coming to his house last night came back to mind. Serenity could see what he was thinking and she said,

"Don't say nothin,"

Rosco jumped in again.

"Say what?"

Before either of them could say something to Rosco, Serenity pointed to an old man walking ahead of them.

"There he go, there he go, that's the man!" Wally knew exactly what man he was. He ran over to the old man, who still had on the same clothes from last night, Rosco and Dumare followed him.

Wally wasted no time jumping on the man. His first slammed into the man's jaw sending him to his knees, where Dumare rammed his knee into the old man's face. The man went down onto his side covering his face with both hands while all three of the boys kicked and stomped him. He only looked up once and once he saw Serenity, he realized what this beat-down was for. A foot blasted him in the eye-socket and he instinctively covered up again. The man was sure his eye-socket was broken.

After a short while, the punches, kicks, and stomps ceased and he could feel his pockets being raided. He didn't dare look up. When he did peek, he noticed the taller dark-skinned one - Wally - had a smaller black gun pointed at him. Wally had gone back late last night and retrieved the gun out of the trash can. The rush it had given him was so addictive and he wasn't getting rid of it until he had another one.

"Take it all man ... please; just don't hit me no more." The old man pleaded. And to Serenity he said,

"I'm sorry baby doll, it was the liquor, I swear, I'm old, I ...didn't mean to hurt you."

"Shut up!" Wally growled as he smacked the pistol across

"Look..." Rosco said, holding up the package he had pulled out of the man's left pocket.

"Let me see." Wally said, taking the bag from Rosco. It didn't take long before Wally knew exactly what it was.

"It's dope." Wally said. The old man saw this as an opening. He hated leaving an ounce of raw Heroin straight from Afghanistan like that, but he'd much rather live to slam another bag. He darted, but none of the kids paid him any attention, except for Serenity who gave him an evil look. If looks could kill he would've dropped dead right there on the spot. He felt guilty, even a little ashamed for what he had done to her but there was no way he could stop to apologize now. The man just kept running.

"Dang, how much you think it's worth?" Dumare asked.

"I don't know, but it's a lot. My mom…" Wally caught himself.

"…this lady I know uses this stuff and she gets little bags for twenty dollars. You could probably fill a hundred of those little bags with this stuff."

"Let's sell it!" Rosco said. That was the smartest thing he had said in a long time, Wally thought. He didn't know just how much it was, but he knew they could make a lot off of it. As Wally put the gun back in his pocket and went to stuff the pack in his waist there was a loud gun shot, they all froze. It wasn't until the second shot that the momentary paralysis wore off and they saw the Pakistani man screaming and shouting something in Arabic with his gun pointed at the old man who was still running towards the end of the block.

The Pakistani hadn't even noticed the kids at first, when he did, he started walking towards them. Again, they were paralyzed like rabbits in fear. Not even Wally could reach for his gun, and even if he could have, he knew it would be no match for the big gun that the foreigner was toting.

The man's eyes dropped to the package in Wally's hand,

"Where did you get that?" He asked. Wally looked up into his pitch-black eyes; they were serious, but not threatening at the moment. The man looked Middle-Eastern, with dark black hair and a clean-shaven face. His face was a sandy color, tight, very earnest, and uncompromising. He looked like he had seen everything at least once and done everything at least twice.

Wally didn't want to give up the work. There was so much he could do with it. He could get away from his mom's house, maybe live in a cheap hotel somewhere, buy some new clothes and sneakers, find a supplier and just keep selling heroin to get by, but by the look on the Pakistani's face, this package was his and he wanted it back. Wally finally spoke up.

"We got it from that old man." He said pointing his head in the direction that the old man had just run.

"I see you were putting it away. So, what exactly are you planning to do with it?" The man asked.

"Is this a trick question?" Wally thought.

"I was gonna sell it; I need the money, we ... we need the money." He said, never one to leave his friends out.

"You were going to sell it just like that?"

"Yea." Wally said not sure exactly what answer the man was looking for.

"Do you know how pure this is? You could cut this 10, 12, 15 times and it would still be purer than the rest of the heroin in this city. So, do you how to step on dope?" The man asked coming closer to the kids.

"No," Wally said, "but I do know some dope fiends that can show me."

The man put his hand up to silence Wally.

"Come to my store later, the one on Cambridge; ask for Ali, my people will be expecting you. I will show you myself. I'll show you all you need to know so you can make some real money. The dope fiends that you speak of will kill for this, or steal like the man you just saw. I'll let you keep this for a percentage and if you do good moving it, I'll give you a job, how does that sound?"

Wally smiled and nodded his head as Dumare came and stood beside his comrade.

"Bring this one too," Ali said, pointing at Dumare. Rosco started moving around hoping to be noticed.

"Not him he, he's too young. And not the girl either, just you two," Rosco looked upset, but Wally would take care of him, he knew that and Wally knew that, and that was all that mattered.

"Seven o'clock tonight, now run off to school now, education is important."

Ali said with a smile.

"What about this?" Wally asked, referring to the heroin. Ali took the package.

"Couldn't let you walk into school with this, I'll hold onto it for you, it'll be waiting for you tonight."

IX

By 1986, the stakes in the drug game were as high as they had ever been for Nasser Saladin. A lot of major political figures had gotten involved. It was the Ronald Reagan era and his CIA agents and the CIA backed rebel army in South America had turned to the drug trade. The link between his CIA-spawned Contra guerrilla army stationed in Nicaragua and a top California cocaine ring headed by the infamous Freeway Ricky Ross was undeniable. This sparked counter-revolutions in Nicaragua and was one of the major players in the 1980's coke boom.

Costa Rica had also gotten involved. Lieutenant Colonel Oliver L. North had been barred from the National Security Council staff when it was discovered that the United States' Contra re-supply operation was now a cocaine ring supplying another ring in California, guns to Iran, and funneling the profits off of the arm's sales to Nicaraguan resistance. The political game was getting shady.

Nasser's homeland was facing similar situations. Reminiscent of that CIA contra-cocaine connection, Afghanistan's plight surrounded the Mujahedin; a military unit that had been set up to take down Afghanistan's opium lords and drive out the Soviet army. In Nicaragua, the CIA had used an

72

army of conservative political exiles to disrupt the revolution taking place there, but they relied on Islamic rebels to drive the Soviet troops out of Afghanistan. Again, the CIA delegate army utilized the drug trade, this time heroin, to raise its treasury. Nicaragua was slowly recovering but Afghanistan was now violently divided and under U.S. occupancy.

The contra war in Nicaragua never got as much media exposure as the one in Afghanistan and where the CIA spent approximately $450 million in Nicaragua, they had more than quadrupled that much with Mujahedin, spending over $2 billion.

Al-Qaeda had now emerged and it was a time of war. These wars included America, the Soviets, and the Golden Triangle, which was one of Asia's two main illicit opium producing areas. This area, which covered over three hundred and sixty-seven thousand square miles, overlapped Burma, Vietnam, Laos and Thailand and also controlled a big percentage of the heroin trade.

Nasser had other things to worry about however, things he considered more important than the petty wars these countries were fighting. All of it was over control of the heroin, just like Vietnam, just like Nicaragua where they wanted control of the coca fields. Gold, oil and drugs; these wars were about economics, not supporting allies, which were the clauses of treaties, this was about money ... Big Money! Nasser instead, sat back and allowed them all to kill each other, the more people that died, the less competition for him.

Across the Atlantic Ocean, Hamid and Luqman had begun college at the State University of New York College in Buffalo. Luqman was majoring in Mass Media Communications and Hamid was studying Computer Engineering. To Nasser, education, and of course wits, was what separated a mastermind from an average hoodlum. His goal, however grandiose, was also to control the world. His plans included more finesse and less martyrdom however. That's why he had men stationed on American soil; men who could intercept military intelligence; men who could occupy post on Wall Street and in other financial institutions; men who could acquire American greenbacks, which were still worth more than most of the world's currencies. Nasser's plan was to wage war internally considering America was much too powerful military-wise to fight through the air or on water.

Hamid and Luqman had progressed a lot over the years. They were no longer little dreamers with delusions of grandeur, they were soldiers with objectives and missions they planned to carry out. Getting Degrees in their respective majors was a job, not a dream. So, they approached their school-work as if their lives depended on it.

Nasser had arranged a meeting between the two boys and a Pakistani named Salaam Akbar, who Nasser affectionately called "his brother from another mother," and his most trusted general. They met at Salaam's restaurant on Delaware Avenue; one block up from the Ansley Wilcox House. When Salaam first saw Hamid and Luqman, the two nineteen-year-old boys didn't look nervous at all. They both looked slightly older than their age and their eyes were intense. They were indeed ready and Salaam liked that

"As-Salaamu Alaikum," Salaam greeted.

"Wa-alakium salaam wa rahmantullah." Hamid and Luqman returned in unison before taking their seats. The restaurant was nice. It reflected the Middle-East as much as the buildings European designed permitted. It served a mixture of Indian, Middle- Eastern, and American dishes. It turned a pretty penny for Salaam, who with his son Ali, owned an array of businesses in Buffalo; a grocery store, a beer, wine and spirits distribution company, a franchised fast-food chain. And that was on top of the kilos of Nasser's heroin they were smuggling into the country from Afghanistan.

"Nice to finally meet you two." Salaam said.

"Nasser has told me so much about both of you. He tells me he is very proud of the progress you are both making in your schooling. I guess he figured now it's time for you both to meet the people you will be working with once you graduate. That is mainly, myself and my son Ali. Ali is slightly older than the two of you, he's twenty-five; he handles the streets you can say. He monitors the mini-market we have set up in the city and also a few other responsibilities for me. You two will start working with him first then you will move up to the higher positions Mr. Saladin has assigned for you."

"He also wants me to inform you that he has a million dollars apiece set up for the two of you in escrow accounts at two separate Swiss banks. The names of these banks and numbers to these accounts will be given to you upon the completion of your schooling. Insha'Allah this will serve as further incentive for you two to do well in school."

Hamid spoke up.

"Luqman and I would do anything to ensure the liberation of our people and everything for the cause. It is a small price to pay for such a big reward."

Hamid spoke fervently and Luqman nodded in agreement.

"Very good Hamid." Salaam said, "But, in the midst of this studying don't allow yourselves to become indoctrinated with western thought, it is poison! A spreading poison passed on by suggestive and rhetorical subliminal messages that fester in the subconscious of those who come in contact with it, slowly eating away at one's true identity, culture, and ideologies until their entire mental being is consumed and transformed into some Europeanized robot. They teach you to memorize in their schools, not to think and they make you believe that one's memory capacity measures their intelligence. Don't be fooled, America and its supporters are one big capitalistic machine that feeds on its own citizens - look at the blacks and other minorities in this country. They also feed on the souls of the impoverished of every other nation stealing and exploiting Africa and Iraq's natural resources, and any other country's resources that they see as lucrative, including our own.

"In the Noble Quran is a quotation from an Orientalist. I made copies for both of you. Take a quick second to read it then I'll continue.

"When the Muslims turned away from their religious teachings and became ignorant of its wisdom and its laws, and deviated towards the contradictory (man-made) laws taken from the opinions of men, there spread in them immorality of character, falsehood, hypocrisy, ill-will and hatefulness increased in them. Their unity disintegrated and they became ignorant of their present and future state and became unaware of what will harm them or what will benefit them. They have become content with the life in which they eat, drink, sleep and compete not with others in superiority."

Once they were finished reading, Salaam made sure they understood then proceeded:

"Politically the agenda is the same. It is total corruption. Just look at this Contra War. The United States, as a matter of policy has abandoned drug law enforcement and has actually enhanced the ability of traffickers to move heroin and cocaine into this country. They are allowing this drug trade to flourish in order to support this Contra movement and support the war."

Hamid decided to add to the conversation.

"I've read that in the sixties, J. Edgar Hoover allowed the drug trade to flourish then also, within the African American community, in his attempt to undermine the Black community's rising in society. A lot of African Americans were beginning to get conscious and henceforth, revolutionary minded and he set out to destroy their communities and the rising of a Black Messiah by allowing heroin to flood their communities.

Senator Jack Bloom, who was actually part of an investigating committee actually confirmed this and released a statement wherein he said that the poor or pathetic justification given by the FBI for using drugs to subdue the African American community in the sixties was because the Black uprising was a communist attempt to undermine America's involvement in Vietnam."

"Bullshit." Luqman blurted out. He wasn't as eloquent as Hamid but he comprehended just as well.

"Bullshit it is." Nasser added with a smile.

"And it's been going on for years but what can you expect from a country that was built on slave labor and corruption but...corruption?"

Again, Luqman broke his silence.

"Allah has destroyed Sodom and Gomorrah and many other wicked nations in the past. America will also have her turn!"

X

Now that Wally and Dumare were working for Ali, things were starting to look up for Wally. Dumare never had a care in the world but whatever his best friend did he did and vice versa.

In two years Wally, at thirteen years old had a stash that a lot of people three times his age would have been jealous of. He was wearing Calvin Klein, and Bally and Polo now instead of hand-me-downs and church donated rags. He never had to worry about food and rarely had to spend money on it. Ali was always bringing them food from his father's restaurant.

"That's Pakistani cuisine right there," Ali would tell them. Wally's favorite had become Sri Pai or anything cooked with lamb and Dumare's was Karahai and anything chicken based. Their days consisted of going to school then running right to the back of the mini-market to grab two packages. Most of the time it was heroin, sometimes crack, and on some occasions it was both.

Whenever Ali gave them some work they would take the two packs and split them in three, making sure Rosco was never left out. Rosco was ten now, still a little wild, but Wally kept him in check for the most part.

Serenity was staying with some foster parents on the Southside. The cops had picked her up on one of those nights Wally couldn't sneak her into the house. One night in particular they were asleep on Wally's porch when the cops approached them. After finding out that Serenity's last name and that she had been missing for almost a year they took her home.

Soon after that Children and Youth took her after it was discovered, Darlene was soliciting her to support her crack addiction. Darlene was arrested for corruption of a minor and a host of other charges and Serenity was placed in foster care, where she stayed in a shelter until a family from the suburb of Williamsville, just north of Buffalo, adopted her.

She and Wally saw less and less of each other. Her foster parents were extremely over-protective of her after they were informed of the atrocities committed against her by her mother. They kept her bottled up, thinking her heart and emotions were very fragile, and not realizing all she wanted was to be with Wally. He was the only person that understood her, that would go out of his way to protect her and make sure that she was alright. That night he spent outside with her beneath that thin wool blanket in the dead winter of last year, when the cops picked her up was a prime example.

Serenity ran away once but Wally made her promise to never do it again, to just stay where she was until he got enough money to take care of her. Then he and she could leave, forever. She gave him her word that she would stay put and wait for him to take care of her like he always did. Patiently, Serenity waited for Wally to rescue her from what she saw as a prison, where she was surrounded by people that thought they understood her and knew what was best for her, but didn't have a clue.

Slowly seasons changed and Wally, Dumare, Rosco and Serenity grew older. The crack epidemic was still at its steady pace if not getting worse. On a national note, it was escalating fast. The Pablo Escobar regime had probably the biggest impact on the coke trade with the help of a few corrupt government officials. Nasser was falling further into obscurity, not because he was being forced out of the way by more powerful dealers - there weren't many more powerful than Nasser Saladin and Afghanistan was still the number one Heroin supplier to the global market - his move to fall out of the limelight was by choice. He didn't want to make the same mistake his predecessor, Hamid El-Qasar had made by getting too big and too exposed. Nasser wanted to die filthy rich but live long enough to enjoy it

"Salaam wasn't lying; there is a million dollars in my account." Luqman said full of surprise as he stared at the numbers acquainted with the account that had been established for him by Nasser Saladin. Poverty makes it hard for you to believe people because most people sell you dreams. Cynicism and little to no expectation is a way to protect yourself.

"Yes, mine too. I did not think that he was deceiving me, Mr. Saladin is a very serious man." Hamid said.

"I am taking Katrina on a trip to Barbados, we leave tomorrow. Mr. Saladin has asked that you take three hundred and fifty thousand to Ali. He hasn't said why but we should just do what he says. I will be back in two, maybe three weeks, make sure you get that money to Ali, and try not to blow the rest of yours."

Luqman smiled, "I'll try."

XI

Buffalo, Ny 1995

His eyes were glued on the old store-front, with its pealing forest-green paint and assortment of cigarette ads and junk-food endorsements. Lottery posters and signs accompanied the ads. The store was suspiciously empty and inactive. Ali's store was normally bustling with customers around this time. It almost looked closed besides the cashier who every so often came from the back to ring up the occasional customer. Once the customer was gone, the cashier would disappear into the back of the store again to do whatever it was he was doing. Whatever it was, it seemed to be more important to him than the business of the period customers who came in for cigarettes and newspapers. His focus on the back of the store's activities probably had something to with the guy in the suit who had gone in a few minutes ago and had yet to come out…

The sidewalk outside was covered in snow besides the trail that had been shoveled for pedestrians who could be potential patrons. About a dozen quarter-gram coke baggies littered the sidewalk, a frozen forty-ounce Colt 45 bottle, an empty chip bag and a losing lottery scratch-off also added to the litter in front of the mini-market.

Rosco watched the store's activity with an Eagle's eye. The nine-millimeter Heckler & Koch P7 he held was burning his palms as he waited to rob the mysterious man that had just walked into Ali's storefront. It was a face he had never seen before and if he could just get this over with quickly without being seen, no one would have to know it was him; not Ali, not Dumare, and most importantly not Wally.

Rosco really needed this money right now. He had hit a dry spot financially and he hoped Wally and Dumare would understand if somehow, they did find out about this. Rosco just knew the suitcase the man was carrying had money in it. That had to be why the guy was in there so long. He was probably buying something big from Ali right now.

Rosco found himself in a conundrum. He knew he was treading dangerous waters plotting on an affiliate of Ali's, knowing it could get back to Wally and Dumare. He had messed up some of their money while they were gone and if he could just do this one robbery, he could replace it without them ever knowing. His brain raced while he staked out the store.

Luqman had left his black CL600 Mercedes Benz running. This was supposed to be a quick drop off before he headed out to Barbados to meet up with Hamid and his wife Katrina, who were already tanning in the hot Caribbean sun. Earlier, upon Nasser Saladin's request, he withdrew a large sum of money from the bank. He hated riding around with such large sums of money - he had close to a half-a-million dollars in his briefcase - but it was a convenience for Ali and Salaam and it was also on his route to the greater Buffalo International Airport by the New York thruway.

Rosco was getting impatient. The man had been in the store for almost thirty minutes now. It was pure chance that he had stumbled across the man. He had been in the store buying Phillies when the man walked in, sharp as a tack in his three-piece suit.

Rosco knew the man was loaded, so he went out to his car and waited. Wally and Dumare were in Barbados with Serenity who was now Wally's fiancé, and some pecan-colored model with world class legs.

"Cuban and black" she had said.

"Damn," Rosco said to himself as visions of her introducing herself then strutting off like she was still on the runway, filled his head. He smiled, then excitement washed over him and the Heckler sent a tingle through his palm and up his arm, the man was coming out...

"Salaam asked me to drop off $350,000 before I left the country," Luqman said glancing back and forth between Ali and his goon, a big burly guy named Izrail who seemed to never speak, Luqman was starting to wonder if he could. Even when Ali asked him questions there was just a slow measured head nod. Izrail was the name of the "Angel of Death," in Islam. The name suited him perfectly.

"OK friend, and I take it he's informed you that my father would handle the real estate issue, correct?" Ali asked. He had already begun counting the neat stacks of fresh money.

"Yes, your father is seeing to that as we speak; so, I was told."

Luqman was prepared to leave when Ali stopped him.

"There is four hundred thousand here; my father said you would be bringing three hundred and fifty."

"I figured you would put the extra money to good use that would be beneficial to the both of us, what good is a relationship if it is not symbiotic right?"

Ali smiled, "I like the way you think."

Outside Rosco bit his bottom lip nervously as he watched the men make their way to the entrance of the store, "C'mon, C'mon..." He uttered to himself. The anticipation was killing him.

Luqman and Ali shook hands.

"May I add that there must be a certain level of trust as well." Ali said and Luqman shook his head in agreement.

"Allah doth command you to render back your trusts to those whom they are due..."

They then walked to the entrance door, Luqman carrying his now empty briefcase and Ali carrying his own, now filled with money. Ali told the cashier to close up for the day.

"Business is slow anyway, bad weather you know…" he said as he and Luqman stepped outside.

Rosco pulled the skull cap down over his face, opened his door, there was the ringing sound that indicated a door was open, he slammed it shut, and ran towards the two men....

"Maybe two weeks or so..." were the last words Luqman would utter before a hollow tip hit the carotid in his neck, the ruptured arteries sent blood squirting like a wine fountain. The dark red drops hit the snow, staining and melting it as soon as they landed. Before he could get his balance, another shot sent his brains splattering against the sidewalk, the look of shock remained frozen on his face, even in death.

Rosco shot at Ali's face next.

"What am I doing?" was all he was thinking as the angel dust and adrenaline coerced him to keep shooting. A bullet grazed Ali's ear and went crashing through the store-front's large windows.

"It wasn't supposed to go down like this..." Rosco reminded himself.

He shot again, missed the chest, hit the right arm, the arm that was carrying the briefcase. Rosco grabbed both briefcases and backed away, still shooting in Ali's direction but missing badly.

The bells on top of the store's entrance clanged as Izrail stepped out, raising the charcoal black Remington Twelve-gauge pump, jacking a shell into the chamber on its way up. The shrapnel exploded at the end of the barrel, with a thunder-like boom that sent a flame followed by a bunch of small metal pellets flying at Rosco. The biggest chunk of shrapnel hit him directly between his chest and shoulder. The strayed fragments flew at his face, two pellets hit his eyeball. The eye went blind instantly.

Blood oozed out of the socket. His entire upper-body had caught some of the blast, and his whole face and torso hurt, he didn't know which wounded area to cater to first. He would have to comfort his wounds later, right now he had to get away.

Lucky for him Izrail had kneeled down to check on Ali, whose arm was bleeding badly. Rosco snatched off his mask so he could cover the mangled eye. He could feel the warm blood rushing out of it too fast. He couldn't feel his left arm. For a minute he thought it was gone. He glanced at it with his good eye just to make sure it was still there... it was.

The briefcase had fallen when the shot hit Rosco's arm. He bent down to pick it up and tossed the ski-mask. He jumped in the car and took a glance at his eye in the rear-view mirror.

"God damn," he said, repulsed by the hideous hole, before he heard glass shatter and felt it hit the back of his head, a piece cut a small slit on the top of his ear, the rear window was almost completely gone. His tires spun out, leaving their dark tread behind in the salted parking lot. He had to get help, but first he had to get rid of the gun, wash up thoroughly, and he had to stash the money...

"What did I just do?"

XII

After a lot of searching, Wally and Serenity found the perfect houseboat to rent while they were in Barbados.

"C'mon babe, it's sexy," Serenity had said after Wally had turned down her first request at sleeping in a boat. She was so happy to be on a trip with Wally again. She was always so busy with college that they rarely had time to spend together. He had paid for Serenity to attend The State University of New York College. Her campus was in Amherst. She just wanted to maximize the vacation, and soon Wally gave in.

"You know it's hard for me to say no to that face, you want to rent a houseboat, let's rent a houseboat, too much ain't enough for my babe."

Dumare and his model friend, Nila, slept in a hotel,

"Where it's safe," Dumare told Wally before he and Nila ventured off to be alone for a while.

Serenity had done a lot of searching for the right boat and finally, she felt she had found it. It was a forty-eight-foot houseboat, so white that when the sun was at its peak, it was hard to look directly at. It had gold trimmings. The owner was on a ski trip in the Aspens and wouldn't be back for another two weeks. Serenity ran over to Wally while he negotiated with the vacationing couple's agent.

"Ooh baby, come look at this bedroom, it's so gorgeous." She said pulling at Wally's arm.

"Give me one second luv." Wally told the agent, who didn't mind at all; the more intrigued Serenity was the better; the more likely the deal was to go down.

They walked aboard the boat. The lower deck's forward eight feet were open and had a golden rail that encompassed it. On the inside, the posh cabin was split into two halves. The front half was the living area. Built-in seats lined the walls, there was an entertainment system, thirty-two-inch television and Panasonic stereo included. There was a dining room table made of marble. At the front was the boat controls with a chair for the driver.

"Well at least we know we won't be fu..."

"See, there you go again,"

"My bad, messing none of that shit... stuff up. I surely don't plan on driving this thing."

Wally was having a real hard time working on his language like Serenity had asked him to. College had her seeing life different, and she knew Wally was smart enough to express himself without every word being a curse word.

"It's cool; we can get somebody who knows how to navigate it for us whenever we decide to take it for a cruise." Serenity said.

"Whatever will make you happy baby." Wally said. Serenity held his face in both her hands and kissed his lips.

"I love you baby..."

"You better." Wally said.

"Ugh, you know that gets on my nerves; say it back.

Wally smiled.

"I love you too ma'ma." Wally said and they continued their tour.

The back was mainly a few small rooms and storage spots. A kitchen, a bathroom adorned with gold fixtures, and a bedroom.

"The sheets are a hundred percent silk." The agent said as Serenity rolled around on the bed.

Wally just nodded and smiled. The man obviously wasn't aware that they had already made up their minds. Wally understood the concept of hustling better than anyone however. It was one of the first times he began to draw up the parallels of his life and the rest of the world's. You had to sale your product; no matter what it was and you had to use a little manipulation and coercion. You had to be quick-witted and make transactions quickly before someone else came and sold their product to your potential buyer.

He laughed inside remembering how Mr. Curtis had explained to him how humans were so evolved mentally because of how social they were and how in any social situation you're going to have mind games and manipulation. People want their way in life so they use whatever machinations they can to get it. Children learn manipulation early on and use their supposed innocence to their advantage. Women use their sexual appeal amongst other things and men use whatever mental prowess or physical powers they have. Life was one big chess game Mr. Curtis had said. And here was the salesmen making a move.

"It does look comfortable." Serenity said after studying Wally's face. He was always thinking so deeply and always so analytical. She just prayed it wasn't to change his mind about renting the boat, she absolutely loved it.

"Come feel how soft this is." Serenity said and when the agent looked away for a second her tongue crept out of the side of her mouth and slowly traced a moist line across her top lip, her eyes were flirty and full of mischief. Wally smiled.

"Yeah, it is comfortable,"

"So, you like it?" Serenity asked though she knew how he felt about the boat no longer mattered. The fact was she liked it and she knew Wally would do anything to make her happy.

As well, Wally knew it didn't matter what he said at this point, Serenity had already made up her mind.

"It's perfect babe."

He turned towards the agent,
"You take cash?"

XIII

Hamid held Katrina's naked body close to his as they laid in the master bedroom of his Yacht; another present from Nasser. Hamid was on his side behind Katrina and she was in the same position, her form melting perfectly into his.

"I wonder what your family would think of me." Katrina said referring to the fact that she was a black woman. This wasn't the first time she had brought this up. They had only been married for two months so far, dating for ten, and she still hadn't met any of Hamid's family besides his sisters who she had gone to college with along with Hamid and Luqman.

"It doesn't matter what they would think of you, I love you, and that's what's important," They met while Hamid was in his senior year in college; she was just a sophomore at the time. After he graduated, they managed to keep in touch, one thing led to another and now she was Mrs. Katrina Morasia El-Qasar, she thought it sounded funny.

"You don't understand Hamid, it does matter to me." Her skin was maple syrup complected, and it had a glow to it. She had the legs and hips of a thoroughbred race horse thanks to the years of

95

gymnastics and track & field in high school. She had a small waist and...

"You know, you have the prettiest breast I have ever seen," Hamid said rubbing one of her thick brown nipples between his finger, they quickly went stiff.

"Stop it Hamid, I'm being serious now. Being accepted by your mother really means a lot to me. You're not embarrassed or ashamed of me are you?"

The truth of the matter was; he wasn't sure how his mother would respond to him bringing Katrina to Afghanistan to meet her.

"Ok, well if you want to know the truth, my mother will probably love you, even more so considering you're contemplating taking your shahada. My Umi is Muslim, and racism is unallowed in Islam. One of the prophet's closest companions was an Ethiopian slave named Bilal. Well, he was no longer a slave once he chose to become the prophet's companion. In the prophet's last sermon, he clearly stated that no Arab was superior to a non-Arab and vice versa. The only thing that makes one man superior to another is his level of piety, or, righteousness. Don't worry so much, she'll love you."

"Ooh, baby, don't stop, ooh," Nila sang and moaned as Dumare slid in and out of her from behind. The warm liquid between her legs made a quiet suction sound every time he entered and a trickle of love slid out and down the inside of her

thighs every time he pulled out. Dumare started to speed up as he got closer to his climax, Nila bit the pillow to numb the pain and muffle how loud she was moaning. Dumare emptied inside of her

"Ummmm, the feeling of you inside of me, that's the best part of sex to me."

Wally and Serenity had just finished their own sexcapade and Serenity now lay with her head on Wally's chest, rubbing his side.

"I was thinking; the wedding doesn't have to be that big. I mean, I know you love me, you know I love you, that's all that really matters, you know?" Serenity said honestly.

"It's up to you beautiful, one or one-thousand people, it's your day and we can do it however you want to." Wally said kissing the top of her head.

"Our day." She said sweetly, making sure to correct him. She looked up into his eyes and his heart jumped, she just stared and it seemed like she could see clear into his soul.

It was something about the way she looked in his eyes that always made Wally drop his guard. Serenity was a tough girl, had been through too much; but at the core she was sweet. She was a romantic who had fallen in love with 18th century romance novels like Jane Austen's Emma, Fanny Burney's Evelin, and Eliza Haywood's Love in Excess. She was extremely thoughtful considering her feelings had been hurt so much that she knew how not to hurt the feelings of others. Tonight, her aura had made the moon seem larger, the stars seem brighter and the air purer. She had on a sheer, red negligee and her skin never felt smoother. Serenity was a mimosa of a woman, sort of speak; refreshing, intoxicating, sweet, tough and the perfect blend of pleasure and pain.

She was a diamond in the rough, there was no denying that. And it was never the quality of her princess cut that was an issue it was the cheap price-tag her crooked appraisers tried to place on her. Unbeknownst to them, there is no value for the invaluable. She needed love more than anything, that and someone she could trust and since they were children, Wally was the only person, male or female, that offered her that unconditionally.

"How could I not make her my wife?" Wally thought.

"You feel like rollin somethin up for me?" He asked, referring to the bud of marijuana he had and the cigar to roll it in. It was another habit she hoped he would one day forfeit. She always felt Wally had unlimited power and potential. He was extremely smart, very calculative; he was a leader, a provider, and these qualities made people look up to him. Serenity knew he had so much potential energy, so much untapped potential, but she promised to remain patient while he found himself; while he found the treasures within. For now, she would support her man no matter what.

"I got you," Serenity replied, reaching for the cigar and green and purple bud on the night stand. Serenity, afraid to ever become addicted to drugs like her mother, didn't smoke weed, and she barely drank alcohol, but she liked to roll his cigars for him. It was her way of saying,

"I got your back even when I think you're wrong."

After his purple haze burned out, they fell asleep while Force M.D.'s sang Tender Love. Wally slept peacefully, he had no idea the opening shots in a war had been fired, and that Rosco was the culprit.

XIV

"WHAT DO YOU MEAN HE'S DEAD?"
Hamid shouted. His yelling scared Katrina out of her sleep.

"How?"

He was crying now.

"How did this happen? How could you let this happen?"

Ali was trying to explain to Hamid the best he could.

"It was an ambush; he just ran up and shot him... twice... it was too late... he died instantly... the money was stolen...four hundred thousand... I'm sorry Hamid...but I know who it was."

The last part was the only thing Hamid cared about at this point.

"Who was it?" He demanded. His anger and sadness were conflated. He wanted to mourn his comrades' death just as bad as he wanted to avenge it.

"He took his mask off when Izrail shot him. The cameras from the parking lot caught his face, clearly. His name is Rosco, his cousin works for me. I don't know how to get in contact with him because I've never dealt with him directly...I know somebody who will though."

"Find out where he can be found." Hamid said wiping away the remaining tears. There would be plenty time for weeping later. Now... it was war.

"He runs with a couple of kids that move work for me. They're good kids..."

"I don't want to hear you say they're good kids. They killed my best and only friend." The backs of Hamid's eyes began to water again. He forced the tears back down before they could fall.

"Well, I don't deal with him, he's my guy's... the kids name is Wally, the one that killed Luqman is Wally's cousin."

"Well contact this Wally and tell him we will not hurt him if he just tells me where to find this cousin of his. Tell him I don't care about the money that was stolen; I just want his cousin."

Ali said "OK", although he knew it wouldn't be that simple. Wally loved and looked out for his people. Ali knew this more than anybody; he had been supplying Wally since Wally was 10. He practically raised Wally and Dumare. He hated the circumstances but he too wanted Rosco dead. For his arm that now twitched from the nerve damage, and for Luqman.

"I'm on my way back home NOW!" Hamid said before slamming the phone down.

Ali's hands were tied. If Wally didn't turn over his cousin he would have to kill him too.

"Damn, I can't get any reception out here."
Wally said staring at his cell phone. He was trying to call Rosco, just to check up on him. He was starting to feel bad for not bringing him with them on this trip. He knew that since a child, Rosco had some issues with people not paying him attention, that and a lot of insecurities. Wally now wanted to tell him to go to the airport and that he would have his plane ticket paid for, but he couldn't get through.

"He'll be alright." Dumare told Wally.

"His birthday is in two months; we'll make sure we do somethin real big for him."

Wally nodded his head.

"Yea, that sound like a plan."

For some reason Wally just wouldn't answer his phone and it was making Ali impatient. Did he already catch wind to what happened and was therefore ignoring his calls? He could've easily gotten the scoop from Rosco. He might have set the whole thing up and conveniently disappeared so he could use Barbados as an alibi. No, that wasn't right at all. What was he thinking? Wally and Dumare went on the trip at his expense. He was the one that told them that they needed some time away.

Ali had suggested the trip for a myriad of reasons. He wanted them to enjoy themselves first and foremost. He knew all about the rough childhoods they had coming up, mainly Wally. He needed them to get away so they could cool off. They sold weight at least 20 hours of everyday; it was only a matter of time before the FEDs got a wire and starting their investigation. Another reason he suggested the trip was he didn't want them to get complacent with where they were at. They each moved a quarter brick of heroin a week, which was good enough to live comfortably, but he needed them to see that even that was shopping money compared to some of the sharks and tycoons he knew. To keep them hungry he wanted them to see that even the Lexus', Audis' and BMWs' they were driving were mediocre in comparison to the Bentleys', Rolls Royce's, Lamborghinis' and Ferraris' the big boys drove. These toys alone were a quarter-million dollars and up. People he knew flew private jets and sailed the seas in multimillion dollar Yachts. He needed to feed their ambitions and higher their aspirations, it would make them better hustlers, and for him, better workers. But that was his feelings then when he felt he needed to look out for their best interest. Now the tables had turned for the worst.

Again, Ali picked up the phone and dialed Wally's number...

He was shocked to hear his voice, then alarmed when he heard the tone that he was speaking in. Hamid was angry.

"Mr. Saladin, I am very sorry to bother you but I need a favor." Hamid said urgently, he didn't waste any time with a formal introduction.

"And what is this favor, Hamid?'

"It's Luqman, he has been killed..." There was a brief silence, a heavy breath of disappointment on Nasser's end. He had seen death too many times to be surprised by it or even slightly emotional about it. In his country death was as common and reoccurring as rainfall. Depression was a luxury he simply couldn't afford. The only sadness he felt was for Hamid. He was young and still immature at dealing with death. Nasser knew it hurt him badly to lose such a close friend however he couldn't afford to see Hamid panic.

"What is it you want me to do?" Nasser asked.

"I need men, twenty maybe thirty men, and I need guns, lots of them..." Hamid was talking recklessly and Nasser had to stop him before he said too much, anyone could be listening.

"Akhi al-habib...my beloved brother, you must calm down. You must be rational. I doubt this is a situation of that magnitude."

"THEY KILLED MY BEST FRIEND; HE WAS LIKE A BROTHER TO ME!" Hamid reminded him in a slightly elevated tone.

"I understand that but you must understand that I don't have the time or the latitude to concern myself with some petty street beef you have with a bunch of hoodlums, nor do you. We have much bigger priorities that need to be attended to, or have you forgotten?"

"No, but..."

"Listen to me Hamid, it is obvious that you are very upset, you should be but don't let anger and revenge be your only driving force. I suggest you handle the situation accordingly. Salaam and Ali already have men in the streets that can handle that. I can't just send that many mercenaries and large amounts of artillery, they would be on me so fast... Hamid, I surely hope that this won't interfere with things." Nasser had suddenly realized that this could become a hindrance depending upon how large the emotional investment Hamid had vested in this death.

"I'm not sure..." Hamid said honestly,

"But I have loyalty towards my friend, and I won't rest until his murderer pays... severely."

XV

"You ever seen some pure black heroin?" Raymond asked his friend Boz', who threw him a disbelieving look.

"Man, it's black as tar, swear on my motha's grave. Ain't nuttin like the stepped on beat up, over-cut shit we get. Ol' Elroy gave me a taste he had got from them Arabs over by Cambridge, whoooo-weeeee, Man I was so high I thought I'd neva come down."

Boz' still didn't believe him.

"C'mon man, you jivin me? Black doo-wop?"

"Hey man, as sure as the grass is green you can believe that to be true baby, seen it wit my own two eyes."

"Hey, hey man, what da hell is ya problem?" Raymond asked as Harold kicked at his feet.

"I'm tired of you goddamn dope fiends always hangin around in my apartments, that's my problem."

Raymond and Boz' got up and walked off cursing at Harold under their chilly breaths as they made their way back out into the frozen streets.

Harold made his way up the steps to the third floor in the building he called his "office". It was run down like most of his apartment buildings were. He owned five of them, all of them being pretty much in the same vicinity, the south-side of Buffalo. His rent rates ranged from forty to a hundred dollars a week. He didn't give his tenants breaks either. Friday was pay day and if you couldn't pay, well you slept outside on the curb. He also ran a bustling after-hour speak-easy uptown.

He was known to keep a pistol on him. A shiny chrome-plated Dan Wesson .32 revolver for when he collected rent. Some people didn't take "get out!" lightly. And people that knew him knew from experience the gun wasn't just for show either, he would use it. As he sat down at his desk with his sack of cash and burning Newport hanging from the corner of his mouth, He sat the revolver on top of the desk, close to his left hand... his shooting hand.

For the most part the room was rather empty, a couple Quaaludes in the desk drawer and a few posters of Playboy centerfolds decorated the shabby walls. An eggshell-colored phone that was almost as old as him; 47. His business cards sat in a tray at the head of the desk and to his right was a rusty metal file cabinet in which he kept deeds, titles, and other important documents.

Hamid had gotten word through Ali that the man who killed Luqman was connected in some way with a local slumlord named Harold Wallace, and that he had gone to see Harold shortly after the shootout in front of the mini-market. Hamid was on his way to pay Harold a visit.

Harold counted his money carefully, throwing the bills into a small safe beside the desk as he went along. He carelessly tossed the change in a pile on the left side of the desk. Harold was an average-sized brown skin man with a lot of gray hair and small beady eyes.

Five minutes into his counting, Harold heard the first-floor door slam shut. His fingers eased around the handle of his .32, and he stared hard at the door to his "office". He hated thinking about death, especially his own. It reminded him that even though he owned a few cheap properties, his final destination was more than likely a pauper's grave, Harold shook his head trying also to shake the somber thought.

The man was a stranger to Harold but he didn't look very dangerous at all. Actually, the slim Arab looking man looked like he wouldn't and couldn't harm a fly. Maybe he needed a place. Harold unwrapped his fingers from around the butt of his pistol, allowing it to once again rest on the wooden desk.

Hamid stepped closer.

"Can I help you?" Harold asked cordially.

"Actually, you can. Is your name Harold Wallace?" Hamid asked, measuredly sizing Harold up like a lion does its prey.

"That's me, now how can I help you?"

"You can raise your hands above your head right now," Hamid said revealing the Beretta nine-millimeter parabellum he was holding in his coat pocket. Harold's eyes grew wide with terror.

"Aww, c'mon man, don't do this to me, what is it, money you want?" His eyes quickly darted to his pistol.

"Too late for that..." he thought and cursed the slowing of his reflexes and dulling of his instincts.

"I could buy you and sell at whole sale value; your money is worthless to me."
At that point Harold figured it was over. There wasn't too much money couldn't buy. This must've been one of those circumstances.

"What? Well, what you want, property? Info? What?"

Sweat was beginning to form on Harold's head; it tickled his scalp then slid down to his forehead. He wiped it away before it could get into his eyes.

"You move again, and I kill you." There was no negotiating in Hamid's tone. Harold quickly got the point.

"Put your hands behind the chair."

As Hamid tied Harold's hands behind him a nasty smell hit him hard in the nostrils, he wrinkled his nose. Harold had defecated on himself and was crying now.

"Coward." Hamid thought as he finished knotting the rope.

Hamid stood in front of Harold and dropped a photograph on the desk

"Do you know this man?"

The picture showed Rosco right after he snatched the mask off. Blood was running from his eye. Harold looked at the photo; he hesitated one second too long. The Beretta smashed across his forehead, splitting the skin to the white meat.

"Yeah... yeah, that's Rosco, my business partner; got stocks you can say in everything I own."

Harold groaned as a stream of blood made its way over the bridge of his nose and onto his lips.

"He drops off work to me too, powder, sometimes hard."

"Someone informed me that he was here, I want to know where I can find him."

"He came in yesterday, real banged up; he had got himself all shot up, asked me to get him a doctor. He kept saying he couldn't go to the hospital, said he thought he had killed somebody. I called one of my friends for him, got him stitched up and he was on his way."

"Where is Rosco now?"

"I swear to God, man I don't know, he..."

Again, the Beretta came down hard on his face, this time striking his nose... it broke with a resonant crunching sound.

"Oh shhhhiiit, aww, goddamn, please man, you gotta believe me, I don't like that joker enough to die for him. I don't know where he at, he usually over on the east side. He probably resting now, you know, hiding out in case he did kill someone, plus he was hit bad, he's probably trying to heal right now... Please, just don't kill me man, that's all I know. I got kids Mr., Kids and a wife."

Hamid walked behind him again.

"Please man, please..." Harold plead. Again, there was a smell, but this time it was urine. Hamid was about to blow his brains out the front of his head when something caught his eye, its silver handle glimmering in the dim light. Hamid grabbed the box-cutter and clicked the razor to the top. Harold closed his eyes tight, by this time he was crying like a baby.

Hamid grabbed Harold's woolly hair and snapped his neck back. With one hard slash that cut tendons, veins and everything in between, he slit Harold's throat from ear to ear. Harold's body began to spasm. His head banged the desk, sending bloody quarters, nickels, and dimes flying every which way. His hands were still tied. He needed to cover the gaping hole in his neck that was pouring out pints of blood but couldn't. Blood was spurting from his severed jugular vein in miniature fountains, spraying the desk, walls, floor and Hamid's coat, the centerfolds' breasts were covered in little red drops of blood as well.

Harold twisted and turned, fell, got up, then fell again. The good thing for Hamid was he couldn't scream; only the sound of regurgitation and more blood escaped his lips. His eyes dimmed until soon, the life in them evaporated, and the obscured pupils stared at Hamid, whose face was unchanged by the death, the blood, and the rest of the gore that would have sent most people to their toilet or the nearest trash can to vomit. His compassion for human life was gone, it had died with Luqman. Right now, he had a vendetta to settle.

XVI

It didn't take Rosco long to decipher the message. He had started a war. When he went to see Harold the next day to pay him for the favor, the cops still hadn't discovered the body. The foul smell of a dead body hit his nose as soon as he opened the first-floor door. When he saw Harold lying on the floor covered in blood from the neck down his first thought was...

"Is it even possible for somebody to have that much damn blood in em?"

The blood had its own distinct smell but death's scent easily overpowered it. Rosco quickly turned around and left the house. Later on that same day, the apartment building turned into an official crime scene as yellow tape blocked out nosy pedestrians, and C.S.I.'s went to work, collecting any evidence they could find. Trucks from different news stations lined the block as their cameras videotaped the scene.

"Probably one of his angry tenets, people say he was a shrewd landlord." Police concurred after speaking with people who lived in Harold's buildings or nearby. And that was what Harold's murder was chalked up as, a case of revenge with no evidence whatsoever. The case remained open but

113

the Buffalo police force was lackadaisical in their approach to solving it as there was no evidence and no motive.

Rosco needed some time to think things through. There was no way he could handle Ali by himself, they had too many men and too much money, and the worst part was, they weren't just Middle Easterners you could spot easily, most of them were guys Rosco had grown up with. Harold was killed not even twenty hours after he had left his office; obviously somebody had connections, eyes everywhere, and was on his heels. He had to get out of town for a few days. Wally would be back in a week, until then he would relocate, and clear his mind. It would all be better when Wally got back; he always found a way to iron things out.

Rosco stopped at his weed suppliers' house before leaving. His supplier just so happened to be his cousin.

"Yo, some guys been asking about you cuz, wussup. They looked real serious too, you ok?" Dominique asked as he passed Rosco a quarter-pound of purple-haze.

"Yeah, I'm good, they probably wanted some work or somethin?" Rosco said trying to down-play the severity of the situation.

"That ain't what it looked like to me. I'm just being real wit chu, them boys looked like you killed somebody man…," Dominique said while he flipped through the bills Rosco handed him.

"Just be safe cuz, you know I love you right, and I'm here if you need me." They shook hands and embraced then Rosco was on his way.

Rosco drove his black Infiniti J30 until he ended up in Erie, PA. There he rented a hotel room for a week, smoked, ate, slept, and thought...deeply. He would be lying if he said he wasn't scared, or at least... worried.

XVII

Dumare hated watching Nila go. She had a shoot to get to in Atlanta but promised Dumare that as soon as she was finished, she would fly back to Buffalo to see him. She kissed his cheek as he left the airport; she was just there to switch flights.

"Somebody's in love…" Serenity said, teasing Dumare as they walked towards their cars.

"Yeah champ, I never seen you like this before…" Wally added

Dumare smiled.

"Nila's a gem man. She knows what she wants out of life and she chasin' it. She got her priorities in order, and it's hard to find somebody as intelligent as her that looks that damn good. Those two qualities don't usually run together you know what I mean?"

"I know what you mean." Wally said, Serenity just smiled.

"If she makes you happy, she makes me happy." Wally said as they approached their cars. They both hit the alarms.

"I gotta go cut this hair off my head." Dumare said rubbing his head. The two weeks in Barbados was showing in the length of his hair.

"Yeah, me too, let's shoot over to the plaza then." Wally said also rubbing his hand through his course hair.

"Sounds like a plan." Dumare said and with that the three of them headed to the plaza.

"Is that them?" Izrail asked, glancing out the window at the threesome standing outside the Chinese restaurant in the block long shopping plaza.

"Yes, that's Wally." Ali said pointing to the trailer dark-skinned one.

"He's like the leader; he's very smart no matter how young he looks. That's his fiancée; right there beside him. The one right there with his back to us, that's Dumare."

As Ali pointed to Dumare, Dumare walked off and headed to the barbershop a few stores down. As he walked into the barbershop, Wally went in the Chinese restaurant while Serenity waited outside, talking to another female who had just walked up.

"Yeah girl, it was so gorgeous, the water, the beaches, the freedom, and I really think Wally's mind is starting to open up. He's starting to realize that the hood isn't all there is to life. I swear he smiled ninety percent of the time." Serenity told Tanesha as they stood in front of Chan's restaurant.

"You lucky girl, Hassan's idea of a trip is to a club on the other side of town." Tanesha said thinking of how small-minded her boyfriend could be at times.

"Wally used to be just like that. He was so narrow-minded at first; it was like nothing existed to him outside of money and the hood. It's so fulfilling to see him finally outgrowing that way of thinking, you know?"

"I know what you mean girl."

"I think he's going to make a great husband." Serenity smiled. And a good father."

Tanesha looked shock.

"You're pregnant?"

She reached out and rubbed Serenity's gravid stomach.

"Yeah, I didn't get to tell him yet though. He's going to be so happy; we've been trying to have a baby for almost two months now, he wants a little girl so bad."

Again, Tanesha's eyes grew wide, but this time with fear as a man approached them. Serenity's back was to the street; she didn't notice the man approaching or the expression on Tanesha's face.

Izrail crossed the street quickly, lurking furtively towards the two girls like a starving cheetah eying a gazelle. His hand was on the inside of his coat gripping the cold nickel-plated .40 caliber that was tucked in his inside pocket. Serenity didn't see him until it was too late. She heard the ruffling of his coat behind her as he pulled out, she turned just in time to see death encased in six and three-quarter inches of Nickel-plated steel. The barrel was pointed directly at her. Tanesha screamed and took off running, Izrail paid her no mind. Wally was just coming out of the store when he saw what was happening.

As soon as he realized what was going on he ran and pushed Serenity. She flew onto her side, her shoulder hitting the hard concrete below, dislocating on impact. Izrail's gun went off, and Wally was raising his arm. Izrail's gun blasted again and now Wally's gun was fully exposed, a compact baby nine-millimeter, jet black, just like the ominous black hole that was now staring directly at Izrail's forehead.

Izrail instinctively hit the ground and rolled behind a car as Wally started firing. Thin sharp pieces of glass from the car's windows sliced at Izrail's face as he slipped and rolled just out of the line of fire. The pieces of shattered glass left half a dozen fine, red lacerations in his skin. He backed away from the car, aiming the Rueger at Wally now, while bullets continued to fly in his direction.

Ali was about to jump out of the truck but ducked back down in his seat when he saw Dumare run out of the barbershop, with the apron still around his neck, gun fully exposed. It was best he just stayed low. It was broad day light, and these boys were wilder than he expected. In fear, Ali watched as his friend was gunned down.

Dumare saw Serenity lying on the ground, lots of blood, and Wally, whose gun was now empty, pulling Serenity out of the way. Wally's eyes were watery. Dumare turned towards Izrail with a look that could only be described as a culmination of anger, hysteria and rage. The barrel of his .44

Magnum exploded repeatedly. Izrail turned from Wally to Dumare, but the flashes from the barrel of Dumare's gun were not only blinding but terrifying. He was only a few feet away, and then yards as he continued to back away. He shot twice then turned completely to run to the truck. He was a foot away from the truck when a slug caught him in the back. It was quickly followed by three more that stood him up, and then left through his chest.

There was a low "ssssssss" sound, like the sound of a tire being flattened. It was the air escaping his pierced lungs as they deflated. His heart beat stalled, managed three more pumps then died out. Izrail laid face down beside the Expedition, a puddle of blood slowly forming around his large body...

Dumare's face was burning but his torso hurt worse. He ran to Wally's side. Serenity looked bad, almost like it was already over for her.

"Go D! GO! We gotta get outta here." Wally said as he carried Serenity's half-live body around the car and put her in the passenger seat. He pulled away from the curb quickly.

"Too many witnesses!" Dumare thought as he ran to his Audi and pulled off just as fast. Both of them headed towards Dunkirk, a suburb outside of Buffalo, they couldn't risk going to a hospital inside the city. If they did, they would be headed for prison as soon as they recuperated, if not before.

Serenity's eyes were wide with fear. The fear of knowing death was now a certainty and that no matter how hard she fought, she couldn't stop it. Wally's eyes had now flooded and the tears began to roll down his face; his baby was hurt.

"You gon be aight baby, just stay with me, stay with me Serenity…please…please baby…don't die on me…"

Wally was pleading with her and he needed a response, some reassurance but the only thing coming from Serenity's mouth was the sound of her choking on her blood. The bullet had hit a major artery in her neck and she was bleeding badly.

Serenity's head rolled to the side and bumped into the passenger side window. Wally was trying to get her to sit up straight, while also trying to keep the wheel steady. He swerved, missing oncoming car by inches.

"C'mon baby, c'mon don't do that, keep ya head up…look, look at me sweetheart…Look at your husband…"

Wally managed a small smile. Serenity looked up at him but her pain was killing him.

"I love you Serenity, you know I need you. You gotta fight; I need you to fight this baby."

Wally was saying all he could to give Serenity the strength to hold on; some incentive to fight. As she looked up at him one last time Wally could see that even through all the pain she was feeling, his pleading voice gave her the energy to somehow feel something else…guilt. She felt guilt and sadness because though she was only semi-conscious of anything besides her pain, she could feel that she was hurting him. Her eyes watered...said sorry...and the light they once retained shimmered; then faded. Her eyelids closed slowly, this time for good...

Dumare pushed his Audi as fast as it would go, steering with only his left hand. He looked up into the rear-view mirror at his burning face.

"Two graze wounds." He told himself as he studied his wounds. The left side of his body right below his ribs felt like a raging inferno. He was using his right hand to cover the pain and the hole that the majority of his blood was leaking from. He looked down at his hand; it was drenched in the dark red life fluid. He grimaced, cursing the pain along with the man that had inflicted it on him.

Suddenly his heart fluttered. It was caused by the panic that filled him as the thought of dying became more and more realistic. Then another spasm of fear shook his heart as he heard the alarming sound of approaching police sirens. The alarm quickly subsided when he realized the police cruisers weren't behind him; they were coming directly at, then, past him at least eighty miles per hour on their way to where the shooting had taken place. Right behind them was an ambulance. The thought of hitting and possibly killing Izrail momentarily appeased him... Then the pain returned.

Everyone was outside of their buildings now that the gunfire had ceased. The barbers, residence, and even the Chinese workers filed out of Chan's to see what was going on. The body-bag was being pulled up over Izrail's head and zipped shut as the lead homicide detective walked over to the crowd to ask questions.

"Alright, who knows what?" He said searching faces to see who his informant would be.

"C'mon now, don't everyone answer at once."

"We don't know nothin and we ain't seen nothin." Said an older man whose whiskey was speaking for him. The detective, understanding his inebriated condition, waved him off.

"C'mon folks, somebody give me something. We got a dead man over here, if we don't get the guy that did this it could be one of your bodies we're wrapping up to send to the morgue."

Still nobody spoke up. Lou Chan and his employees began to walk away. They wanted nothing to do with this. They knew Wally, Dumare, and Rosco since they were kids, they liked them but they also feared them now that they were older. Wally's gang was notorious in these parts. You don't keep a lock hold on the drug trafficking in a city for so long without some ruthless violence. Violence and muscle was all competitors respected.

"Man you don't understand, we gotta live here, work here, sleep here, you don't."

That summed up the sentiments of everybody at the scene; nobody was talking, some out of fear, and some out of love for Wally. Here was a young man who had paid some of the elders' rents when they were behind and took the neighborhood kids on trips to Disney World all at his expense. When was the last time a cop did that? The detective grew impatient and began interviewing the entire block individually. Still, nothing. Nobody knew a thing and those that did weren't telling. The closest thing to a lead the detective got was from an older lady in her mid-sixties who from across the street had watched everything from her third-floor window.

"From what I could see that man there got just what he deserved, shot that poor little girl like that, in cold blood."

Wasn't much to work with, but he did warn all hospitals in the area to be on the lookout for a young woman, probably between seventeen and twenty-five. She was the victim of a shooting and may know something. She may even be accompanied by the shooters involved in the murder.

"I don't know." The middle-aged Italian woman told the officers at St. Paul's Hospital in Buffalo.

"Some young man; a young black man. He asked me to please take his sister to the hospital. I think she was already dead. He said he didn't want her to be left in the streets like something worthless. I couldn't just leave her; it would have been on my conscience forever."

The detective could tell the lady wasn't lying. And she was already shook up enough. He decided not to drill her; instead, he got a description, a sketch composite, gave her his card and let her go home.

Dumare felt faint. He dizzily staggered into the emergency room. His entire left side was covered in blood. To his legs his body felt three hundred pounds heavier. The loss of so much blood started to get the best of him and finally he blacked out, sliding to the floor. Nurses quickly went into action. The stronger male staff lifting him onto a gurney...oxygen mask...IV's...pressure on his chest...his eyes were open just enough to see the blinding white lights, then, black...

XVIII

Wally entered the Hospital in Dunkirk approximately forty-five minutes after Dumare did. His detour in Buffalo to change clothes, get rid of the gun, and drop Serenity off on that woman had cost him those extra minutes.

"Serenity... Damn…"

Once he located Dumare's room, the doctor stopped him at the door.

"He can't have visitors at this time." He said levelly.

"Well can you at least tell me if he's gonna be alright or not, that's my brother sir."

"Oh, I'm sorry." The doctor said, his suspicions evaporating only slightly.

"Well, your brother is in a coma right now…"

Wally looked away; the doctor paused. When Wally refocused his attention, he continued.

"He was shot in the head."

Again, Wally winced. It was a good thing that he had changed shirts. The blood from Serenity would have forced the doctor to ask the question that was already burning inside of him;

"You wouldn't happen to know how this happened, would you?"

Everyone liked to play detective at one time or another, instead however, the doctor chose to remain professional and not allow his suspicions force him to make premature accusations.

"He will be bedridden for a few weeks, maybe longer depending on how long it takes the comatose state to subside. If it..."

He stopped himself; the young man had obviously experienced enough grief. Wally understood though, if it ever subsided.

"Another bullet punctured a few internal organs. He lost a lot of blood."

Wally could see a bag filled with red liquid right beside a bag filled with anesthesia. On the other side of his bed were a bag for his feces and a bag for urine both connected to tubes that went under Dumare's gown and into his bladder. Wally shook his head, disgusted, all of this for what? Izrail was Ali's right-hand man, and Ali loved Wally and Dumare like sons; he had just sent them on a trip.

"What the hell is going on?" He thought then suddenly a barely audible voice grew louder in his ear. The doctor had been mumbling while his mind had drifted.

"His brain is our main concern."

"Is he going to be brain damaged?" Wally asked seriously.

"We don't think the injuries were that severe, however it is still too early to ascertain that certainly. There's no real way of determining until he awakens, then we can actually analyze his brain activity, you know to determine whether or not it is channeling thought properly. Only then will we be able to assess just how much control he still retains over his mental faculties. His motor skills haven't been damaged; he walked himself into the hospital before swooning in the E.R., so paralysis is out of the question, thank God.".

"Yeah, Thank God."

Twenty minutes later Wally was finally allowed to enter Dumare's room. He sat in the chair next to his comrade. Dumare looked noticeably smaller, not in stature but in aura like most men do when reality humbles the ego. Dumare was at the mercy of immense pain and possibly death. He looked weak, fragile; almost childlike again. Wally put his hand over top of Dumare's.

"Yo D man, you gotta wake up for me bro, you know I can't do this without you."

For the second time in less than two hours Wally was asking, begging, one of his loved ones to hold onto life, for him.

"Rosco need you too man, he need both of us, he crazy, but the dude love us, sometimes you more cause you baby him up." Wally laughed, thinking about Rosco.

Wally had called him on his way to the hospital but Rosco's phone was turned off. He thought about calling him again, but things had gotten hectic with Serenity and now, Dumare. He did wonder where Rosco was; it wasn't like him not to answer his phone.

Wally was still talking to an unconscious Dumare when Dumare's mother and father arrived at the hospital. Wally made sure to call them as soon as he got there. Dumare's mom had pure hate and disdain in her eyes as she walked straight at Wally. He stood up and her open hand came across his cheek with a loud smack. Wally grabbed his face and looked up at Mrs. Makita hurt and surprised. Tears were pouring down her face, as Curtis restrained her.

"Stay away from my boy Wally, I mean that, you stay away from him you hear me?! We do everything we can to keep him out of those streets and all you do is pull him back into em... I hate you for this!"

Her words cut deeply at the tissue of Wally's heart; his stomach dropped. He glanced over at Curtis with tears in his eyes.

"I'm sorry Mr. C, you know I didn't mean for this to happen, I still don't know why it..."

"I know, I know Wally. Just go out in the hall son, I'll be right out there to talk to you. Just let me get some time in with my son."

Wally walked out as Curtis whispered something to his wife.

"I'm sorry Mrs. Davis." Wally managed before he stepped out of the room. Dumare's saddened mother said nothing; she just cried into her husband's shirt then sat beside her son.

Sitting alone in that hallway, Wally felt horrible. He knew the truth when it came to him and Dumare. Dumare made his own decisions. Still, what Mrs. Makita had said was partly true, Dumare was smart and thoroughly provided for; he didn't need the game. Wally was the only reason he ran the streets, the only reason he was in the hospital right now. Curtis came out, and Wally tensed up.

"Listen Wally, my old lady's just a little shook up right now that's all. She's already saying how sorry she is for saying what she said to you, she feels bad. You know she don't hate you at all, she loves you like her own. I always told her, it ain't the fact that you're hurt that matters, it's how you take it. She let her emotions get the best of her, trust me; she's very remorseful right now. I know what you and my son are into. I was once into the same thing. I do wish I could get y'all to understand, it's safer ways to apply your hustle, some may not always be as lucrative or as fast, but their much safer, I also know that a man is going to be a man. Let's make this clear, I want you two to just leave this alone, whatever you do the bullets lodged in my son's skin won't disappear and if they do the scars they left wont. But I got a feeling you're already driven by revenge, I know you've already got plans for whoever did this to my son, and since, no if, there's no way I can stop you, just be careful, please, I don't want to lose my sons."

XIX

After leaving the hospital, Wally made the long, lonely trip back to Buffalo. It was one of those trips where his subconscious had to navigate because his mind hadn't been on the ride the entire time. Once he pulled up to his house, he couldn't even remember the ride there.

He had a lot of questions that needed to be answered, mainly, why the hell did Izrail kill Serenity? And why would Ali order the hit? Izrail never made a move without Ali's consent. So, Ali had to be at the bottom of this, but why?

Then he began to think about Serenity and how he had to drop her off in such a rush, was that heartless? He glanced up at his sad reflection in the rear-view mirror,

"Nah, that was all I could do at the time, she was already gone, what good would it had done to get locked too."

He would have to give her a private burial. It hurt to think that his baby was lying dead on some cold metal slab in a morgue, with an ugly incision stitched into her torso. He had to locate somebody close to her that could identify her at the morgue, maybe Mr. Curtis. Wally would fund the entire thing.

"Damn, Serenity's gone, Dumare's fighting for his life and consciousness, and Rosco's missing, so that's what a free trip to Barbados cost?"

Rosco made his way back to Buffalo reluctantly. He had spent the last week lost in his weed smoke and lines of cocaine. If he wasn't over-sleeping due to nervousness, he was stewing over the drama he had caused. He knew exactly what Wally would say.

"You didn't have to do it that way, you know I would've made things right."

Rosco knew Wally too well, and he had heard this all before, it was also all he heard while in Erie.

As Wally headed towards his apartment, he scrutinized the surrounding area a little more scrupulously than usual. The lady that had dropped Serenity off at General Hospital was probably questioned by detectives; that was almost a give-in. She had probably supplied them with a description and sketch of him; he had to be extra careful. He drove past his place twice, then finally parked and headed towards his door.

Wally lived in a completely paid-off condominium in Orchard Park. The architecture of the building was modern design. The complex had just been constructed in 1992 by a New York City developer with deep pockets and a lot of vision. The exterior and interior were like a palace compared to what Wally had grown up in.

He had a compact but stylish kitchen with stainless steel appliances and granite counter tops, a small dining area right off of the spacious and decked out living room, a nice-sized bedroom, also lavishly furnished, a bottega with large windows facing the north, and a study filled with books donated to him by Mr. Curtis who encouraged him to read as much as he could to enlighten himself.

"Reading shatters the mental shackles colonialism has placed on the original man's mind and way of thinking. Reading is the first step to true liberation because it allows one to become a free and independent thinker, this freeing of the mind will eventually lead to the freeing of the physical. Every black man needs to know this."

These were Mr. Curtis's words before giving Wally over fifty books by authors like Cheik Ante Diop, Naim Akbar and Chancellor Williams.

Wally also had a 52-inch TV, a stereo system with surround sound that brought life to every room in the condo when it was on. He kept his Lexus 430 parked in a private garage up the street. He had another apartment, almost identical to this one, in Connecticut. It was a gift given to him by Ali's father, a man he had never met face to face. He just got the keys to it a month ago. He and Serenity had spent two weekends there before all this happen. They had photos of them together there and being as though she liked it in Connecticut so much, that particular condo was starting to become home and this one in Orchard Park was slowly becoming the getaway. There were two reasons he couldn't go there now. He wouldn't be able to stand it without Serenity, and Ali was more than likely an enemy now.

Wally opened the door and hit the lights. His eyes scanned the apartment searching for the slightest sign that someone had been there. Everything seemed to be just how he had left it and once he was satisfied that nothing was out of place, he relaxed a little. He tossed the keys in the tray that sat on the end table closest to the door and locked the door behind him.

He walked to the kitchen and grabbed the half-fifth of Patron off the counter. He twisted the top, smelled it, it was strong, just what he needed. He poured the clear liquid into a tall glass and drowned it. The tequila burned his throat. His face tightened. Still, he filled the glass back to the brim and downed it again. After that he grabbed a bottle of Merlot and poured himself a glass, carrying it with him to his bedroom where he grabbed his stash of marijuana. Somberly he made his way to the front of the condo and sitting down in the living room; he began to unroll his Vanilla Dutch Master, emptying the tobacco into a trash bag. He licked the cigar paper, filled it with the Red-Hair Sesimelia, twisted it, and then dried it with his lighter.

He grabbed the remote to his stereo and hit the power button, in twenty seconds Ron Isley was singing … "Drifting' on a memory... there's no place I'd rather be, than with you..."

One minute later, weed clouds filled the adjoining rooms and Wally was deep in his feelings.

XX

Rosco walked timidly to Wally's door, twenty minutes after Wally did. He knocked twice. Inside, Wally was scrambling for his Bryco 59 semi-automatic .380 – small - but this would be close range.

"Who is it?"

Rosco's heart beat hard when he heard Wally's voice. You can prepare for something mentally but you won't know you real reaction until the situation is actually in front of you.

"It's me Wally…" Rosco said. The door opened a crack.

"Damn man, you had me worried, where... Yo, what happened to your face?" He said noticing the eye patch. His eyes drifted as his mind made a few lighting quick calculations.

"Yeah man, that's what I gotta talk to you about…"

Wally stared at Rosco speculatively. It was like he was having a premonition; he could predict what Rosco was about to say, he just prayed his intuition was wrong. He stepped aside and let Rosco in.

"What happened Rosco?" Wally asked, in an accusing tone.

"Damn... dig Wally, I'm a keep it real wit you, when yall was outta town, I messed some money up. So I hit this dude comin out of Ali's store..."

Wally's face transformed, his nostrils began flaring and his eyes closed to thin slits, he waited to hear the rest.

"Man I swear to god G, it wasn't no way for me to know who this dude was, he could've just been a customer or somethin'. I saw that the opportunity so... Look, I never saw dude before, and I was hurtin,"

"What is your idea of hurtin? You got over two hundred grand in da stash alone, I could've taken care of the shit... Man, forget all that, what did you do?"

"I killed him, and I shot Ali too, he was in the way, I got this shit on my eye, my eye is blind forever." He pulled the patch back to let Wally see the sealed mess that used to be an eyeball hoping the sight would soften Wally's chastisement.

"The buckshot, it spread and hit..." His next word never filled his mouth, only the taste of a warm, and copper tasting liquid as blood from his lip rushed into his mouth.

"Do you know what you did...do you know what you started?"

The words were pounding into Rosco at the same time punches were. Wally's fist caught him right in the right eye almost leaving him completely blind. They wrestled for a minute knocking nick-knacks and Wally's glass of Merlot to the rug. Wally managed to untangle their arms and punched Rosco square on his jaw, Rosco grunted loudly and his jaw hung limp, it was dislocated.

"You got Serenity killed!" Wally said as he choked Rosco's neck as hard as he could, so hard he thought his thumbs would plunge directly into his Larynx and esophagus. Rosco was gagging and crying,

"I'm sorry, I'm sorry…"

Wally finally snapped out of his rage, he was killing his cousin. He released his hands and fell back up against the sofa, tears in his eyes now as he thought about Serenity.

"Why couldn't you just wait til I got back?" He paused and exhaled.

"You know I would've made things right…" He looked hurt, even more hurt now than before because now that he realized his fiancé's death was caused by his irresponsible cousin.

"Wally, I'm sorry G, I'm so sorry," Rosco continued to weep. Again he had killed somebody he loved, worse yet, somebody Wally loved, the only thing that truly made Wally happy.

"I…I just wanted to show you that I could handle shit while y'all was gone, but I messed up again."

"You damn right you messed up, you killed my wife, and I couldn't even tend to her death properly cause we was under the gun. I just had to kill somebody…now me and D might be wanted for murder. Ali probably after me, Dumare's in a coma, Mrs. Makita is flippin on me! All of this cause of you and ya lack of judgment."

Wally hung his head after telling Rosco what his stupidity had caused. When Wally raised his head, Rosco had his .380 in his mouth.

"What the..." Wally lunged at Rosco. Just as he pushed Rosco's elbow there was a loud blast as the gun went off.

XXI

On the other side of town Hamid was growing very impatient. Ali told him where he may find one of the boys.

"It's an old apartment tenement over by the West Shore apartments. You may be able to find them there."

Ali had offered to go along but Hamid wanted to do this himself. It was his friend they had killed and he would be the one to avenge that death. He wanted no one stealing that glory from him.

Hamid had made his way to the apartment building Ali sent him to and now was waiting impatiently for one or all three of them to show up. He looked so out of place, this Middle Eastern man in a dirty crack house surrounded by crack addicts and dope fiends. The dope fiends were shooting and nodding, nodding and shooting. They were completely oblivious to Hamid and his odd presence in their shooting gallery. The crack addicts, however, were very alert and very aware of the fact that it was strange that this Arabic man, clean in his dress and grooming, and obviously not peddling anything, was in this apartment. He was beginning to worry them but they had more important things to worry about, like, refueling the high that though very euphoric only lasted a few minutes. No harm no foul they concluded regarding his presence. They too had once been clean and groomed so maybe he was here to begin his ending.

Finally, Hamid asked if anyone knew where he could find Wally, Dumare, or Rosco. He had flashed a picture of each man, then, a crispy hundred-dollar bill as a gratuity for any information anyone could offer. Most of the addicts knew that, that particular hundred-dollar bill could cost them their lives and kept quiet. One, braver - or greedier -than the rest, approached Hamid.

"At least one of em is gonna come by, they gotta drop the youngster out in the front some work off, he gettin low."

"Would you please tell him to come inside, I need to speak with him." Hamid said calmly. He was referring to the "youngster" the older gentleman spoke of.

"Alright." The man said before stepping outside. Against his will, Dorian, one of Wally's youngest workers came inside. He had no heroin and didn't feel like being bothered but he decided to see what the problem was.

"Do you know when Wally will be here?" Hamid asked.

"Nah...when he gets here, he gets here...This is what yall called me in here for?"

"Well do you have a phone number I can reach him at?" Hamid asked ignoring the hostility in the youth's tone.

Dorian laughed.

"Are you crazy? A number? Man, I don't even know you. Matter fact who the hell are you, and who let you in anyway?"

"I m a good friend of Wally's and my friend Raymond let me in." Hamid said smiling at the addict he had given the money to.

Dorian looked at Raymond with a look that showed his dissatisfaction. For all he knew, this guy could've been a cop and Raymond, greedy for money, could have just caused a whole lot of problems.

"Yeah, well if you re such a good friend, why don t you have his number, why don t you just call him?"

Hamid was all out of patience. He wasn't about to argue with a twelve year old boy who knew nothing more than the ghetto matrix that had raised him. Hamid grabbed for the boy but Dorian pulled out of his clutches. By the time he had tussled his way out of Hamid's grip he had a .25 caliber Bryco pistol pointed at Hamid's eyes. Hamid however didn't even flinch. He struck like a cat. In one quick motion he had removed a surgical scalpel from his pocket and cut Dorian's face open. Hamid had struck so hard that Dorian had actually felt the blade against his bone. Blood poured from his face and the pistol dropped from his hand. He began to shake and before Hamid could tell him to strip he passed out from a mixture of pain and nerve trauma. His face had literally been unfastened and the sound and feel of razor against his bone had been the eeriest thing he had ever experienced. He had gone into shock and fainted.

Hamid stripped Dorian's shirt and jacket from his skinny torso leaving the bloody boy exposed from the waist up. Looking over at Raymond and the rest of the addicts that littered the crack den Hamid said,

"I want you to give Wally a message for me."

No one spoke, just watched as Hamid sliced Dorian's torso open with the bloody scalpel leaving his organs and entrails completely exposed. A dope fiend who had risen from his nod just in time to see the horrific mutilation vomited on the floor beside him.

"Hooolyyyy shit!!! Hey man, what da fu'…O my god…"

Raymond couldn't form a cohesive statement, just a bunch of expletives that expressed his shock. His cursing turned mute quickly as Hamid stalked towards him with the deadly scalpel pointed at, and almost touching, the bridge of his nose.

"Please man…oh Jesus…please don t kill me man…"

Raymond was trembling with fear. His eyes were clinched tightly closed and his left sock was absorbing a hot stream of urine that had begun to make its way down his leg. Hamid touched his face with the scalpel. Dorian's blood was now on his cheek as well as his hands.

"Do you get the message?" Hamid asked sarcastically.

Raymond nodded very slightly as not to accidently bump the scalpel.

"Good. Now make sure you give it to Wally. Tell him to contact Ali immediately."

Hamid turned to leave, only to see that the only people left in the house where he and Raymond. His victim was still on the floor covered in blood of course, but Dorian was no longer Dorian. Dorian was now no more than a soul returning to its origin and a corpse headed for rigor mortis.

"Hey man, Hey Dumare man, some dude came by the spot today, terrorist lookin' joker. He killed Dorian man, slit him from neck to naval…Hey this dude crazy, strait-jacket crazy! He said get in contact wit Ali but I suggest you get in contact wit a travel agent and get the hell outta town. I know yall tough but this dude scared the piss outta me…literally. I'm just relaying the message. Yall must've really pissed em off. I'm out!"

XXII

The errant bullet flew directly up into the ceiling; causing a cascade of dry wall and insulation to rain down on their heads as Wally continued to wrestle with Rosco for control of the gun.

"Let it...GO!" Wally said, finally freeing the gun from Rosco's grip. Rosco was eighteen years old now but the way he balled up and cried made him look younger. Wally just hugged him tightly and assured him that he would take care of everything, like he always did.

"I just keep messin up Wally. I killed Petey, now Serenity. I got D hurt, as long as I'm alive I'ma just keep hurting people that I love, aint no reason for me to live if that's what it's gonna be..."

"I don t wanna hear that. I still love you, no matter what. You the only blood I got and I'ma take care of you. Didn't I promise you that when we was younger, that I would always take care of you, that I would always be there for you?"

Rosco nodded his head but the gravity of the situation was making it too hard for him to keep it erect.

"Did I ever break a promise?"

Rosco nodded but this time a head nod wasn't good enough for Wally. He needed assurance that

Rosco knew he would take care of this and that no matter how angry he was he would never turn his back on his family.

"Look at me." he said raising Rosco's head.
"Did I?"
"No, you know you didn't Wally."
"And I never will. We gon make it through this one just like we made it through everything else; together."

Wally was never allowed to be weak. He was always looked to for strength, courage and reassurance. He would have to mourn the loss of Serenity, the love of his life, later.

That night, Rosco filled Wally in with all the details. He told him about Harold and even managed to form a smile when Wally told him that Dumare had murdered Izrail.

"Obviously we gotta lay low for a while. Everything happened in broad day light. D's gonna heal fast, he's a soldier. When he does, we'll handle this situation accordingly then get out of this town for good."

Wally sat back and studied the space in front of him.

"I was ready to branch off and do my own thing anyway; I made enough money for them over the years."

As Wally had hoped for, Dumare healed rather quickly. No matter what lifestyle he lived, Dumare was still a very conscious young man. He fasted once a week and "Ate To Live" as he was taught according to a nutritional book given to him by his father. The book was written by Elijah Muhammad and stressed discipline in one's eating habits and the importance of limiting one's self to one full-course meal a day. He went to the gym regularly and no longer smoked or drank alcohol. His body was in ideal shape to fight trauma.

Dumare had regained consciousness shortly after hearing his mother's voice in the hospital. A week after being shot and nearly killed he called Wally to relay the message he had gotten from Raymond about Dorian's death and the nature of the man that was pursuing them.

"Whoever he is, he's crazy Wally, seriously. Raymond told me he cut Dorian open from neck to navel with a scalpel, left him there to bleed to death, guts falling out and everything."

"Yeah, Rosco said he slit Harold's neck ear to ear." Wally said, taking a brief second to imagine how excruciating Harold and Dorian's deaths must have been.

"Harold?" Dumare asked unsure of exactly who Wally was talking about.

"You know, the slum lord Rosco deals with, own the apartments and speakeasies…"

"Oh, Harold…wow…"

"Yea, I guess he tryna scare us or something."

Wally sounded like he had nerves of steel but he felt a hint of nervousness inside. Any man this ruthless had to be killed. There was no negotiating with a ruthless killer like the man who was stalking them.

"For what reason though?" Dumare asked.

"Why is he after us like that, there's a lot of dudes with a lot more paper out here. Did one of us offend him personally or something?"

"Apparently Rosco messed up some money while we were out of town. He saw some guy comin outta Ali's store holding a briefcase and figured it was an easy robbery. He didn't want us to know he messed up the money so he stuck the guy up. I guess the robbery went bad; whoever the foreigner was, he wasn't playing! He wasn't just some cookie-cutter businessman. Rosco had to kill him and ended up shooting Ali. The dude that killed Dorian and Harold is a friend of his and he won't stop until he gets his revenge."

Dumare shook his head and tried to process all the information Wally just relayed. He wanted to be angry with Rosco and probably should have but once you know and understand the nature of a person or thing it's hard to get upset with their behavior.

"Well," Wally said taking Dumare's silence as a sign to go on.

"Afterwards, Rosco was feeling real bad about the whole situation and all the drama he caused, crossing Ali, getting you hit, getting Serenity…"

It was hard for Wally to say killed.

"I spazzed on him for what happened to Serenity and that just pushed him over the edge. I looked away for a second and when I looked back he had his gun in his mouth."

"He tried to kill himself?" Dumare asked shocked. He now felt sorry for Rosco.

"Yea, he actually squeezed the trigger but I reacted just in time."

Wally shook his head as his mind quickly relived the event.

"No matter what Wally, he needs to understand the affect his choices have on all of us; that the decisions he makes hold ramifications on, not only himself but me and you as well."

Wally was still suppressing a lot of rage and resentment.

"I know, I know but yo, you gotta forgive him, you got to. He don t know what he be doin sometimes; his mind don't think far enough ahead to see repercussions. No matter what, he family and we gotta love him. I mean he almost got me killed and I still love him, I know you do too. We gotta charge this to his mind, not his heart. Damn; he really tried to kill himself though?"

"Yea, scared the shit outta me." Wally admitted.

"Well, just keep a close eye on him. We gotta make him believe this aint all his fault; we gotta claim some of the blame. If not, this'll just perpetuate that disorder he has, that post-traumatic stress... You remember what he went through with Juanita after Petey died in that fire…"

"Yea I know, she blamed him over and over and he had that survivor's guilt hanging over his head already."

"Exactly. We just gotta be careful with him that's all. Plus, this is the game we signed up for… there's a lot mishaps on the way to the top; wherever that may be…I could make a bad move, you could make a bad move…we just have to focus and be more aware…"

Now Dumare was contemplating his own existence and reasons for continuing in the self-destructive lifestyle he was living. He was intelligent and had good parents; parents that would jump at the opportunity to help him get away from the street life and in a less paying but more rewarding career.

"Yea you right, as always." Wally said.

"So let's just get past this if we can. Tell Rosco he still my family, I love him, and nothing but betrayal would make me stop. It was an accident, a major one, but an accident nonetheless."

"I will. But D, whoever this dude is, he bringing it right to us, it's about time we flip the script. I never been a good runner and I never liked hide and seek."

"More or less." Dumare concurred.

"So what I'm thinking is; they really just want Rosco. He's the one that killed their friend and he's the one that robbed him. They really don't want us but they'll go through us to get to him if you know what I mean. So what I want to do is just have Ali meet me somewhere, anywhere, and I'm sure he'll bring the guy with him."

Dumare was all ears. He would have to pay close attention for any holes in Wally's plans. It was his position.

"When they show up, I won't be there but I'll have the homie Bruce follow em once they leave. Shouldn't be that hard if he do it right. And it should lead us to where this dude is staying."

"Be careful." Was all Dumare said.

"Don't worry, I got it. You just worry about getting some rest and getting better."

XXIII

The streets were so deserted that the silence seemed anything but silent. It had transcended sound and became an eerie, ominous feeling that shrouded the streets of Buffalo. There was an unusual absence of cars and flowing traffic and although it was chilly, the lack of people out and about was suspicious. The drug addicts were scared to be seen right now after word spread of what happened to Dorian at one of Wally's spots. Landlords were just as nervous after hearing what had happened to Harold. There were a thousand rumors and theories floating around but only one concrete fact. There was a war going on and nobody wanted to be caught in the crossfire.

Besides that, vice cops and local detectives were putting the pressure on people looking for any information that would help with the investigation of the four murders. A special TASK force had been formed including DEA and FBI agents from other parts of the country to help with the investigation. Though it would be hard to link the slum lord's murder to the twelve year old boy found two days ago and even harder to link both to the young woman and Middle-Eastern man's murders, something was telling them that all four murders were connected in some way. Because of this hunch, they were interrogating any and every one. This left the Johns angry because the working girls were afraid to be outside to be harassed and badgered. The dope fiends were angry because the dealers were all lying low as well. And Hamid was extremely angry because Wally still hadn't surfaced.

"I think it is because he is a coward! That, or..."

"Trust me, this kid is very smart." Ali warned.

Hamid who he could see was starting to underestimate Wally. They were still awaiting Wally who had called Ali earlier to arrange a meeting.

"I was going to say that." Hamid said in his own defense.

"That or he's playing some type of game."

Hamid was becoming more and more skeptical about the meeting and why they had chosen to meet on Wally's terms.

"So they don't want to come out of hiding? Well I'll make sure they have no choice." Hamid grunted as Ali started the car and headed towards the house Hamid was staying in.

"Three fifty-three Berry Lane" Bruce said as he watched Ali pull off and away from Hamid's house.

"I could hit him right now." Bruce said. He was anxious as he watched Hamid walk up the walkway to his front door. Hamid took a look around the neighborhood then walked inside.

"A woman met him at the door. I couldn't see her that good, she was garbed up, what you call it her Hijab…She was small though, petite, maybe five one, five two, a hundred-ten, a hundred-twenty."

"Alright. If you can hit him then hit him, if not, don't worry about it, the information's enough."

"Well, it's like Mr. Rogers neighborhood out here so it would probably be best to get him at night. I'ma make my way back."

Bruce hung up and started his engine. He took a quick glance in his rearview and noticed a black Suburban making its way up the street. He wrote it off as no threat considering how slow the truck was moving. Throwing the car in drive he didn't notice the Chrysler pulling in front of him until it was too late. It was the same Chrysler he had followed to Kenmore and it had parked perpendicularly in front of him. Bruce's heart started racing. It didn't take long to put two and two together. He slammed the gear shift in reverse and stepped on the gas but it did him no good. He only slammed into the side of the black Suburban that had now pinned him in his parking spot. Bruce quickly jumped out of his car and let off his entire magazine; half at the Suburban and half at the Chrysler. He had hit nothing but car and truck not one person in either vehicle was hit.

Bruce's heart dropped as the back doors to the Suburban opened. He struggled with the extra magazine he had in the inside pocket to his jacket to no avail. AK rifle bullets pierced his torso. He struggled for breath but it was useless, both lungs were pierced. He dropped, first to his knees then flat on his face. There was a loud crushing sound as his skull cracked against the concrete.

"What is going on?" Katrina cried as she and Hamid lay on the living room floor listening to the barrage of gunshots right outside of their window.

"Nothing. Just keep your head down." Hamid ordered.

When the shooting finally did cease Katrina stared accusingly at Hamid. She knew he had something to do with the shooting. He seemed to calm, almost ready for it. Not to mention he had been acting extremely strange lately.

"Tell me what is going on Hamid!" Katrina demanded.

"Nothing."

"You can't keep saying nothing Hamid, gunshots are far from nothing." Katrina was about to break down from fear.

"I'm scared Hamid. You've been acting so strange lately - so withdrawn - and now this. I'm just afraid and I wish you would tell me what is going on."

Katrina's fear consumed her anger and tears began to flow. Hamid wiped her tears with his thumbs and hugged her close to himself.

"I want you to pack up a few things and stay at your mother's house for a while."

Hamid still never gave an explanation.

"What?" Katrina asked.

"At least until things calm down."

"What? What about the baby?"

Katrina placed her hand on her stomach.

"Don't worry, this will all be over before the baby is born." Hamid said. He placed his hands over hers to comfort her and the baby growing inside of her.

"Don't worry, this will all be over before the baby is born, I promise."

Hamid placed his hands over Katrina's and laced their fingers. Her hands were trembling and seemed smaller than they really were.

"I'm scared Hamid, what is this about? Can't we just leave the country? Or at least the state? We have more than enough money."

"I just can't do that Katrina." Hamid said releasing her hands.

"Why not?" Katrina asked. She was so desperate now. She knew the longer they stayed the worse things would get.

"Loyalty." Hamid said.

"What about me? What about the baby? What about being loyal to us?"

"I have to handle this Katrina. It's no longer up for debate."

"But…

"No more! Now pack your things, I'll take you to your mother's house."

That night, Hamid took Katrina to her mother's house in Amherst and departed for what he said would be an indefinite amount of time. Right now he was in a war, something he knew all too well. He had grown up Afghanistan; all he knew was war. His neighborhood was a war zone; his playgrounds and schools as well. Dilapidated warheads, landmines, machine gun munitions and shell cases; these were the images that inundated the young mind of Hamid. A beef with some local hoods from Buffalo was nothing in comparison to the wars he had seen and lived overseas. After a few moments of recollecting his past in Afghanistan he made his way back to Kenmore, grabbed his things, and then headed to a hotel in Buffalo.

Wally was disappointed when he found out that his plan had backfired. He felt guilty for getting Bruce killed as well.

"Damn." He groaned as Rosco hung up the phone. The shaking of his head was a signal that he still hadn't reached Bruce.

"He still aint answering." Rosco said. That had to have been the twentieth time he had called Bruce s phone.

"He's dead…" Wally said flatly. He was shaking his head, staring into space. It was the first time he truly pondered what he was caught up in and why?

"What now? What do we do now Wally?"

"I'm going to that house." Wally had a determined look on his face.

"The house where the dude stay? That aint smart." Rosco was surprised at himself for questioning Wally.

"It is, because they definitely won't be expecting someone to show up after what just happened. As long as the place is not crawling with cops, it might be a chance that they'll still be there."

"I doubt it." Rosco said

"I got a feeling." Wally answered.

The next day Wally got up bright and early. He left his condo at four thirty a.m. and pulled up in front of Hamid's house on Berry Lane exactly two minutes after five. From outside he couldn't tell if the house was empty or not. There was a blue BMW parked out front but it was almost right between Hamid's house and the neighboring house so there was no real way of telling who the car belonged to. So, instead of making a move too soon, or, the wrong move, Wally just waited.

XXIV

"Mom, I'm gonna borrow your car for a minute." Katrina said. She was standing over her mother who was still asleep at the time. It was a little after four thirty a.m. and Katrina had to make a quick run back to the house. She had forgotten what she thought was very important, her brand-new Enzo Angiolini purse. She knew Hamid would probably be upset with her for going back to the house but she needed her I.D. and credit cards. She would only be there for a minute and right back to her mother's.

"Where are you going?" Katrina's mother asked her while yawning at the same time. Her eyes were barely open.

"Just gotta run back to the house and grab my purse real quick. I'll be right back."

"Ok baby, drive safe." That fast Katrina's mother was back to sleep and Katrina was headed out of the house.

Wally glanced at his watch; five eighteen and still, no motion. If Hamid was going to leave it was going to be early he reasoned. Unless of course he had left last night. With that thought Wally turned on the ignition in his car. As his hand drifted towards the gear shift, he noticed a car coming towards him. He turned the car off quickly and ducked in his seat. He slouched until he was eye level with the dashboard.

The car was beige; 1994 Lexus. The driver was a woman; the woman. Wally watched her closely as she stepped out of her car scanning the area suspiciously. As he watched her all he could think about was Serenity. These people had taken her life. Still, he questioned if he would be able to do the same to this young woman who was most likely innocent to all that was going on.

Wally waited until she was completely in the house before he got out of his car. He too glanced around as he walked towards the house. An eerie feeling crept up inside of him. Bruce had lost his life in the same manner. It looked as if people were just starting to get up for work. A man jogged by in a gray sweat suit but he never once looked Wally's way. Wally could see movement through the windows of a few of the houses and realized he would have to act fast. Standing at the door he prepared to open the door but before his hand reached the knob it began to turn. Wally ran to the side of the house.

He could hear Katrina locking the door, her keys were clinging, that was the best time, her back would be to him. Wally ran up behind her and jammed the gun hard into her back. Katrina gasped.

"You scream and I swear to God I'll kill you. Now turn around slowly and walk."

"Please don t kill me...I'm pregnant." Katrina plead.

"Wally was stunned. Pregnant? A flash of Serenity's face appeared…his child…gone…he couldn't harm this woman in anyway.

"Just walk."

Katrina was petrified but she complied.

"You see that car over there?" Wally pointed to his car.

"That's where you're walking to, don't scream, don't run, and don't get cute. You do and I'll kill you, it's that simple."

When they got into the car, Wally tied Katrina's arms and legs up and sealed her mouth with a gag and tape. She sat there calmly. The only sound she made was an occasional whimper and sniffle. They rode out to a wooded area outside of Kenmore and Wally pulled off the road.

"What's your name?" Wally asked after removing the gag from Katrina's mouth.

"Katrina…"

"Ok Katrina…Your husband and his friends murdered my pregnant fiancée, He slit a twelve-year-old child's…"

"Those murders?" Katrina asked in horrid shock. Of course, she had heard about the woman killed by the Arab man in Buffalo, and the child, and the Landlord…it was the biggest thing on TV right now.

Wally just nodded his head, a tear forming in his eyes as he glanced at Katrina's mid-section.

Katrina on the other hand was shaking her head back and forth in disbelief.

"Oh my god...I've been sleeping with that man......"

"I'm not gonna hurt you, I'm not an animal. But you have to go and if I do ever see you around here again, I can't promise something won't happen to you..."

"Go back? I would never go back to that man; I would never want my child to know that man...that monster...I don't know what I'm gonna do. He knows where my mother stays, all of my things are in his home..."

Wally was thinking her situation through as well as his own. Up until she revealed her pregnancy, Wally's intentions were to hold her as collateral until Hamid surfaced. Rosco wanted to kill her. He wanted to avenge Serenity's death and he felt it would put him back on good terms with Wally and Dumare.

"Here, take this number."

Wally gave Katrina a torn piece of paper and a pen and she wrote his number. It was risky of course but Wally was a good judge of character. This girl wasn't screaming, fight, or trying to get away. She really just wanted to be far away from Hamid after discovering the nature of the cruel beast that lived inside the man, she always felt was gentle, sweet and mild mannered. She had no idea he was Dr. Jekyll and Mr. Hyde.

As Wally dictated his phone number to Katrina, he found himself blinded by a corona of beauty that had now eclipsed her somber aura. She was beautiful and Wally felt bad for admitting it.... but he felt it...amidst the heavy amount of anxiety he felt the connection of forlorn spirits slowly making their way to the serendipitous discovery of destiny...his mind entertained a fantasy...

As Katrina wrote down the numbers Wally dictated to her a warm feeling began to melt the ice that was forming around her heart. She had no idea who Wally was but he was very handsome, she had no idea what he did for a living, probably shady if guns and killing were involved but there seemed to be a heart inside of him...and now she would be single...and he had lost his child and fiancé to the hands of her fiancé and friends...and he was hurting...and she was hurting...her mind entertained a fantasy...

Rosco watched from his car in the distance. Why was it taking Wally so long to get the girl out of the car and take care of her? They had to send the message back that they weren't afraid. That they were willing to go just as far as Hamid had. Just then Wally's car started and he was headed back to Hamid's house in Kenmore.

"I promise he won't be there. I just need to get my things...I'm never going back to that house." Katrina said as she thought about the controversy that was surrounding Hamid. He was probably a suspect in these murderers and he would be receiving a life sentence or the death penalty when caught. She had no time to waste waiting for those events to unfold, it was time to escape and start a new life.

"I trust you." Wally said. Katrina's eyes penetrated his soul. She trusted him as well.

"I know..." Katrina admitted and her stare locked a second longer than it should have. They both felt the awkwardness, but acknowledged its origin in attraction.

Wally pulled up to the house and watched as Katrina ran inside. Just then a car pulled up behind Wally's...too suddenly! Wally reached for his weapon and watched his rearview closely. Rosco opened his door and Wally's tension evaporated.

Wally pushed the lock switch and Rosco climbed into the passenger seat. He was enraged.

"What the hell are you doing Wally? Are you crazy? Don't tell me you fell for this woman!"

Wally's mind drifted... Had he?

"What about Serenity man, these people killed Serenity!"

Wally put his head down. Part of him felt he had let Serenity down; the other part knew she was pleased with his decision. She wouldn't have wanted him to take that innocent girl's life. She wouldn't have wanted him to continue this war. She would ask him to swallow his pride, no matter how disgusting it tasted, and move away from it all. Start over, leave the streets alone, and put his beautiful mind to use in another field; one more productive and less self-destructive. And she would also want him to eventually be happy with a woman who pleased his heart.

"Nah, this shit aint over Wally, we aint goin out like that."

"Goin out like what Rosco? Why are you here?"

"You think I woulda let you come out here by yourself? You need somebody to watch your back just like me and Dumare do."

"Yeah but…"

"But nothing Wally, and you was about to let this bitch live."

"She didn't do anything Rosco…she's innocent…until I told her she didn't even know what was going on man, I swear to God."

"Neither did Serenity but that didn't stop them from killing her. Man, forget that, they gotta feel the pain you felt."

"Nah man, it aint worth it."

"Yes, it is. Eye for an eye, tooth for a tooth."

"Rosco end of discussion. She's a nice girl man and she's pregnant I don't want it on my soul…that karma…I wouldn't be able to live with it you understand. All of this man, I'm tired, I'm just tired…"

Rosco understood.

"So what are we gonna do with her?" Rosco said sounding defeated.

"Nothing. She wants to get her things and get she and her mom far away from here. She had no idea dude was that crazy."

"And you believe her?" Rosco asked.

"Yea I do man, she's not like them…"

"How do you know?"

"Cause I feel it…"

"Yea? I bet…so what else you feeling?" Rosco asked interrogatively.

"I don't know…" Wally admitted.

XXV

Islamabad, Pakistan

Salaam met with Nasser to discuss the progress of their mission.

"Believe me, there are many places in the United States where security is scarce. They have laws set up to protect the privacy of their citizens. These laws allow a lot of things to go unnoticed. This goes for planes, cruise ships, trains, everything."

Nasser just listened, closely, after hearing what he wanted to hear he interjected.

"And what about our boys, have they handled their little beef yet? Or at least come to their senses and realized that we have much bigger issues at hand. Once we gain control of what we plan to these hooligans we'll be at our mercy anyway."

Salaam shook his head no.

"Hamid is like a man possessed. This vendetta has completely consumed him, and Ali has vowed to see to it that this score is settled. He too feels betrayed, and violated by these perpetrators."

Nasser retorted angrily,

"Then it's final then, neither of them no longer has my support or backing. We have hundreds of men in the states and though I love those two in particular, I will not allow my association with them to disrupt my plans and eventually bring about my demise."

Salaam put up no argument.

"Ali is my son but sadly I feel the same way. We haven't spoken in weeks and I have the growing feeling that this lack of communication will become permanent."

"Then I would say that you are a very smart man who has his priorities in order. We cannot allow anything to stop us, not even family."

Salaam nodded in agreement.

"So, how are things at home?" He asked.

"It is becoming increasingly hard to tell apart the U.S. operatives who are being sent to investigate us and the delegates of our CIA friends. For the most part though, all is well. Our boys are making sure that all weapons being sent to the rebels here, who seem to hate us even more than they do the Americans, are being diverted to my army and fellow opium lords."

Nasser smirked smugly. It was the smile of an arrogantly complacent man who felt as though he couldn't be touched. To Nasser, the world was already his.

"Our boys in the CIA also make sure at least one of every three dollars sent to supply the mujahedeen so they can destroy us, finds its way into my pockets. The CIA gets their cut and we get ours and the mujahedeen, well they just get used! The US is using these rebels and they don't even realize it. Their Congress gave their approbation for Pentagon advisors and hundreds of stinger missiles for this group of rebels, but their support has sparked many different terrorist groups and much bloodshed. America's problems are much bigger than us now my friend."

Nasser patted Salaam on the shoulder, they both smiled and Nasser added,

"Now they've got Al-Qaeda to worry about."

Hamid studied the note closely.

"What is it?" Ali asked.

Hamid paused, he was obviously enraged so Ali prepared himself for the worst.

"They have Katrina…"

"What now?" Ali asked

"We go pay Wally a visit!"

After Wally ditched his car he called He jumped into Rosco's and they headed to Wally's apartment.

"I just want to run to my spot really quick, grab grab a few things, then we goin away for a while."

"Where to?" Rosco asked. The idea of a trip was actually exciting to him.

"Denver." Wally said without hesitation.

"Colorado? Damn, why so far?" Rosco asked as he made the turn onto Wally's street.

"It's way too hot out here for us right now, we wouldn't be able to get at a dollar even if we wanted to. Ali on us, the D's is on us, plus it's a lot of wrinkles in my life right now and I need some solace and time to iron it all out."

"I feel you." Rosco said. He was parking the car right in front of Wally's condominium.

"What about Dumare?" Rosco asked before Wally got out of the car.

"He already knows. We'll go pick him up soon as I'm done here."

Wally looked up and down the block before opening his door.

"Give me five minutes."

After Wally left the car, Rosco took the cigarette from behind his ear and pressed in the car lighter, waiting for it to heat up.

"How much further?" Hamid asked. He was growing impatient.

"The next block over." Ali told him as they paused at the stop sign, then rode slowly up Wally's street, parking behind a black Infinite, it was the more luxurious Q45 model.

"I like those cars." Hamid said pointing at the Infiniti.

"Yeah, they're nice." Ali agreed, before noticing that someone was in the car. Whoever it was leaned down and lit something. Hamid could see that it was a cigarette as the head turned diagonally towards them. They both watched the driver closely. The tint on the back window was making it hard for them to see who the driver was.

"Which apartment is his?" Hamid asked, only slightly glancing away from the car in front of him.

"It's that one right there." Ali said pointing at Wally's condo.

Upstairs, Wally was packing only things of importance into his suitcase. A few pairs of jeans, shirts, 2 Beretta 9's, both with 13 shot clips, a Heckler and Koch MPS Sub Machine gun and a Kevlar Vest with ceramic inserts. He took the money out of his safe, $364,230, enough to cover his expenses once he got to Denver and enough to get him some nice work once he got dug in and found a good connect.

He taped the cash to his waist after making a layer as flat as possible, then wrapping it in plastic. He put the girdle over top of it and double-checked the condo. As he walked back to check his room one more time a loud blast stopped him dead in his tracks. Another blast and then another. Wally ran to the window facing the front of the condo.

Rosco lit the cigarette and put the lighter back into its hole in the ashtray. He took a puff, the cigarette stuck to his finger when he tried to pull it from his lip then fell on his lap.

"Oh shit, oh shit!" He panicked, and brushed frantically at the cigarette. The burning, orange tip broke free from the unburned tobacco and began to burn through his pants. He opened the door and jumped out of the car still brushing at the flame.

"That's him, that's Rosco!" Ali said jumping out of his car. He ran up to Rosco and shot at his neck without hesitation. He missed his neck but hit his shoulder. Rosco turned to run but the next shots hit him square in the middle of his back. The bullets landed in his spinal column. Rosco went down hard unable to move.

Wally watched from upstairs as a third shot went off. Hamid had shot Rosco in the back of his head. Wally knew Rosco was dead, there was no denying that. He watched as Ali and Hamid turned towards his building and started for the door. Wally had finally seen the face of his enemy. He took in all of Hamid's features then ran towards the back window.

Wally could hear them running up the steps as he climbed out onto the fire escape. He threw the suitcases to the ground below and hurried down the metal steps.

Ali was in the condo by this time. He saw the open window and ran directly to it. He peered down to locate Wally.

"Here he is." He said and began shooting down at Wally, who was kneeling down to pick up the suitcases. The bullets were barely missing him, chipping small pieces of pavement not even inches away from his body. Wally grabbed his luggage and ran towards the next block where he would be out in the open and surrounded by witnesses that might make Ali think twice about killing him right now.

"I'll get the car." Hamid said as Ali ran down the fire escape after Wally. Wally was running full speed without daring to look back. He was mad at himself for not carrying one of his Berettas in his coat pocket, but he had planned on a smooth getaway; a slight miscalculation. He could hear a car speeding up behind him, he looked back…Hamid…Sh….!

Right as the car was about to ram him, he turned off into an alley. The tires were screeching to a halt.

"He's reversing." Wally told himself as he turned back onto a main street. People were looking at him as if he were crazy as he darted past them with his suitcases swinging.

"Hurry up, hurry up!" Hamid said as Ali got into the car. He pulled off again in a hurry but it would be a very long time before he would see Wally's face again.

Heavy breathing…
"Blew his brains out D, by the time I saw em it was too late. I'm over on…"
More heavy breathing…
"I'm downtown, the bus station, we gotta go now!"

Wally's chest was still heaving heavily. He listened to the voice on the phone then spoke again.

"Yeah I saw his face… I'm positive, I lost em…"

"Aight, just hurry up…"

"Okay, Peace."

Dumare's Audi pulled up two minutes later, Wally jumped in and they headed straight for Denver.

XXVI

New York City, NY 2011

It was a morning like any other morning for Cynthia Jackson. She woke up at five-thirty, brewed herself a cup of Starbucks coffee, toasted two slices of wheat bread, and turned on the 13 inch color TV that sat on the granite counter in her kitchen. She reached over and grabbed a green apple from the fruit basket and listened as the news reporter reiterated last night's news.

Cynthia worked as a secretary for a bond brokerage firm. It was a nice paying job that afforded her the $80,000 Victorian Town House she and her two children lived in on Long Island. It was quite a step up from the shabby apartment she had grown up in in Philadelphia, Pennsylvania. A lot of hard work and determination had taken her from the rough streets of North Philly to the quiet suburbs of Long Island. She considered herself blessed.

Cynthia was spreading apple jelly on her toast when her nine year old son Trevor poked his head around the corner.

"Morning mom." He said sleepily.

"Good morning baby." Cynthia returned with a smile. Trevor walked in the kitchen and Cynthia greeted him with a light kiss on his forehead.

"So what'll it be this morning, Fruity Pebbles or Coco Puffs?" She said enthusiastically, trying to liven Trevor up, he had to be to school in an hour.

"Coco Puffs." He said, a little more spirited, a smile slowly creeping onto his face.

Cynthia turned to pour Trevor his bowl of cereal when a high-pitched voice scared her, causing her to spill the small brown balls all over the counter and floor.

"Mommy, mommy," Cindy screamed running into the kitchen and jumping up onto a stool.

"You know what today is?" She asked both sweetly and exuberantly. Cindy was adorable. Seven years young, she was an exact replica of her mother, only smaller. Her skin was cinnamon brown just like Cynthia's and her eyes were the same almond shaped and amber color. Their hair was exactly the same texture but instead of the bob Cynthia sported today, Cindy donned two afro-puffs that were now loose because of sleeping on them.

"Of course I know what today is silly girl, it's Tuesday." Cynthia said teasing her daughter.

"No mommy, I know it's Tuesday, but it's something else too," She said sounding slightly irritated but still sweet.

"Umm, the 11th..." Cynthia said still dragging her joke out.

G.O.D.

"Mo-mmy," The playful smile was still brilliant and her head was tilted to the side, but Cindy was getting frustrated.

"It's my…"

"Birthday." Cynthia finished. She walked over to Cindy and tickled her side.

"You didn't really think mommy would forget your birthday did you?"

"Nooooo," Cindy giggled. Cynthia pulled a present from beneath the counter. Cindy tore the wrapping to shreds. Even Trevor's eyes were wide with curiosity as he watched little pieces of red and gold gift wrap fall to the floor.

"Oh, thank you mommy," Cindy said revealing a pair of pink and white Barbie skates.

"Tonight, we'll go the skating rink and try them out, what do you think about that?"

Cindy jumped up into her mom s arms,

"I love you mommy."

Not too far away in nearby Staten Island, Bob Messinger, CEO of the same Bond Brokerage firm where Cynthia was employed, was also preparing for work. Bob was a 42-year-old man born and raised in Staten who loved two things; his family and golf. Before making the daily trip to Manhattan to work, he drank the rest of his Florida orange juice then kissed his wife on the lips.

"Now don t be late tonight darling, you know Robert's soccer game is tonight. It's their championship and he'll really be looking forward to seeing you there." Bob's wife said after he removed his citrus-tasting lips from hers.

"I'll be there, I promise."

One more kiss and he was out the door, headed for work.

Cynthia kissed Trevor and Cindy good-bye at their school and drove towards Manhattan for her 8 hours of work. Cynthia's SUV weaved slowly through the congested New York traffic and just when it seemed like she would never make it to work, she arrived at the 110-story building where she made her living.

Bob Messinger passed Cynthia's desk just as she was settling in.

"Hey Cynthia,"

"Hi Bob," Cynthia said cordially. Bob dropped a stack of papers about a half an inch thick onto Cynthia's desk. She knew what was coming next.

"Do you think you could have this typed by eleven?"

"I have a meeting at noon and this is very important."

He formed it as a question, but Cynthia knew what Bob was really saying was,

"Have this typed by ten-thirty."

"I'll get right on it." She said. At exactly 8:48, while Cynthia typed there was a noise, a loud noise that rumbled the glass that surrounded the offices.

Cynthia and Bob both stared out of their respective windows. For Bob, it all happened too fast for him to even realize what it was, but for Cynthia, it was a moment of slow motion and heightened senses. She smelled fear and danger, heard the whistle of the approaching plane clearly, and with eyes wide with terror she watched as a plane's nose crashed through the window, glass flew and bricks collapsed. Dreadful screams filled the office and soon the roof collapsed onto her head and she heard no more. As flames engulfed Cynthia's office, she, Bob, and thousands more would die that day; innocent people. One thousand five hundred children of employees in Cynthia and Bob's firm alone lost their parents that day. The crash was heard around the world.

At 9:03a.m., approximately 15 minutes after the Trade Center's North tower was struck, hijackers of a United Airlines flight headed straight at the South tower, and just 56 minutes after the United crashed, the South tower crumbled to the ground. The North tower collapsed 29 minutes later, at exactly 10:28.

"Rick, there's complete pandemonium down here!" A news reporter shouted, covering her ears to block out the sounds of chaos behind her.

"You've just watched as the second of the Twin Towers was destroyed by planes claimed to be hijacked by terrorists. The kamikaze-like suicide

attacks have completely destroyed the World Trade Center. There are dead bodies everywhere. Some mangled bodies clearly visible and others yet to be pulled from the rubble. People have plunged to their deaths from more than eighty stories high."

The reporter paused and glanced away from the camera. Then returning her gaze to the camera she said.

"We've just gotten reports that the Pentagon has also been hit. Allegedly, one hundred and ninety people were killed in the plane and on the ground. Again, one hundred and ninety believed to be killed at the crash at the Pentagon. Wait,"

She glanced away again. The news just kept coming.

"We have also received word that a fourth, I repeat a fourth plane, also hijacked by terrorist, has crashed in a field southeast of Pittsburg, Pennsylvania. Once again, nineteen terrorists have crashed hijacked, commercial airliners into the World Trade Center in downtown Manhattan, the Pentagon in Washington D.C. and a plane that may just have missed its mark, crashed in a field right outside of Pittsburgh."

The reporter continued to describe what had just rocked America. It would become the worst attack on American soil since Pearl Harbor.

Rescuers searched for survivors, days after the crash. More than five thousand people were missing and over five thousand and five hundred people died in the attacks. On September 15th, The President announced that the nation was declaring war. He warned U.S. citizens that a sustained fight would be needed to defeat terrorist and he identified Saudi-born Osama bin Laden, believed to be operating from Afghanistan, as the prime suspect in the attack.

XXVII

Clear across the Atlantic, Salaam, Nasser, and Hamid - who over the past few years had found himself back in good favor with Nasser - were secretly celebrating right outside the city of Baghdad, while the people of the middle east - seeing this as a cause for celebration - paraded the streets, thankful that the United States had finally felt the effects of blood being shed on their own soil. They weren't concerned with whether or not this had been a ploy by the American government, an inside job or an actual scheme by terrorist, they were just happy that America had finally gotten a dose of its own medicine. Their city, once a beautiful city and center for learning for scholars around the world had been destroyed in the Persian Gulf War.

In the seventies, Baghdad had experienced a great period of growth and prosperity thanks to the increase in the price of petroleum which was the city's largest export. New water, highway, and waste structures were built all to be destroyed by Iranian and American forces in Operation Desert Storm. To the citizens who had watched the demise of their city, there was a sense of satisfaction as the same people who had destroyed their metropolis felt the same pain.

For Nasser and his constituents, it was so much more enjoyable because it hadn't turned out to be the Pyrrhic victory they had planned for. With the heat mainly on Osama bin Laden and Al-Qaeda, Nasser and his heroin cartel could rest easy as long as they stayed out of sight and out of mind. Nasser knew the way to beat America was economically, he smiled as the Yen and the Euro began to rise in value as the greenback declined. America's currency was slowly losing its value. His plan was expedited by the attacks.

As expected by Nasser, on October 7th the US and Great Britain, backed by an international coalition against terrorism, launched missile and air attacks against Afghanistan, the first offensive actions in what Nasser and Salaam expected to be a very long war.

Ali was supposed to meet with Hamid, Nasser, and his father in Afghanistan in two days. Today he had to shut the store down, for good, head directly to the bank and have his savings transferred to a bank in the Caymans. Afterwards he had to head to his stash houses to pick up the rest of his money then he would be gone for good.

Ali grabbed whatever little money was in the store, glanced around it to double check and make sure he had everything, then he stepped out and locked it up. He was pulling the metal cage down in the front when he felt a hard jab at his back followed by a voice that told him not to move. Ali went to speak but the pressure against his back grew and the voice, this time more aggressively, said,

"Just shut up and get in the car!"

The burglar turned Ali around.

"And put cha damn hands down." Taheer told him.

Taheer was one of Wally's workers and the brother of Dorian. Not only was he in pain because Ali and his people had killed his brother but he wasn't thrilled at the fact that Ali had driven Wally out of town. Wally always took care of Taheer's problems so he figured he would repay him. Even worse they had killed his brother.

Ali turned to see his robber's face. He noticed that the boy's eyes were darting back and forth and that he was probably just as nervous as he was, the difference was, Taheer had cold steel pressed into his back and he was naively unarmed. Ali complied. He climbed into the back of the Jetta where another armed youth was sitting and the driver pulled off. They had Ali lead them to one of his stash houses where he handed over fifteen ounces of uncut heroin and over $200,000 in cash.

"There, you have what you want, now let me go."

That would be the last words to come out of Ali's mouth as a bullet cracked through his skull and landed in his brain. He dropped; dead weight. Taheer kicked Ali's feet back into the house and pulled the door closed. Ali's reunion with Hamid would never be.

Hamid decided to stay in Afghanistan so he could be with his family for a while. It was something he hadn't been able to do for a very long time. His mother was fifty-two years old now, and though she still retained much of her youthful looks and vigor, Hamid wasn't sure just how long he had left with her. She was becoming very ill. Her cancer was getting the best of her.

The trip had also given Hamid a chance to get back into his Islamic roots. He had truly strayed. He had sought out the consultation of a local Imam and the dialogues he had been having with this sheik was restoring his faith. His biggest question was the concept of God, after traveling the world and being exposed to so many different views.

"Some people say God is an abbreviation for Gomer-Oz-Dabar, a Hebrew term meaning wisdom strength and beauty." Hamid expressed to the sheik.

"Others say it is no more than an acronym for Gold, Oil and Drugs which is what most people, most notably, Masons and members of the Illuminati apparatus worship."

The sheik pondered these two concepts. He hadn't come in contact with this train of thought but it made much sense to him.

"Well, what I can say is that there is one God, one Universal, transcendent, omnipotent God. In Islam his name is Allah, which closely resembles the Hebrew Elah in both spelling and pronunciation. Most philosophers and all theologians have a concept of God but it is their polytheistic views of God, or their anthropomorphism of him that lead them astray. They misinterpret the image of the sustainer and creator of life. These people that you say worship God in the form of gold, oil and drugs will make sacrifices for these things which include but are not limited to the murdering of men and women both innocent and guilty."

Hamid thought about the war he was in with Wally. It started over money.

"People will commit haram or forbidden acts like selling drugs, *riba*, or usury, or businesses that deal in interest. These interests create debt that further impoverishes the already poor."

Hamid thought about Nasser and his opium business. He thought about the drugs Ali supplied. These drugs were destroying the people who consumed them as well as the people that distributed them.

"Then, where you have these religions or ways of life that promote shirk, or attributing partners to Allah, or where people are free to worship prophets, money, their desires; you see people doing just that. They worship idols, these golden calfs, and are lead astray from worshipping the one true God. The force that creates the atom, drives the wind, produces the rain, impregnates intelligence in the bee to produce honey that cures sickness in man and is palatable to the taste."

"In Hinduism, Brahman is the all-pervasive, eternal, absolute reality in which all things have a beginning and end. However, he is a personified entity that shares divinity with Vishnu and Shiva. So he is no longer one force but three abstract forces that work against and with one another.

"In Christianity, Jesus the Christ – peace be upon him – is the incarnation of God. How this is seen as possible is beyond my understanding considering he prays to God to save him from the pains of the cross and the burden he must bear, the Devil tries to trick him as if he doesn't recognize the creator that barred him from heaven, he sleeps, and eats and bleeds, and somewhere forgets that he is God because he continuously prays to himself. He also says the works he does he cannot do without the father. But if he and the father are one there is no need for distinction or demarcation. So people have begun to pray to him and worship him which takes away from the praise of the one God. In making a man worthy of praise it has led to the praise of Saints, Popes, Mary – peace be upon her - and so many people whose duty it is to serve God, not to be God.

GOLD, OIL AND DRUGS

"In the Yoruba religion of West Africa, which is followed by over ten million people there is one supreme God, Oladumare, there seems to be the worshipping of spirits and idols. In Buddhism it seems God does not exist. There seems to be an atheist spirit as there is no God that bestows blessings and administers punishments. There is only the action of man, Karma, and there is no eternal afterlife, only reincarnation where one transforms in life form. Jainism seems to be the same where there is no God, only liberated souls who achieve the status of immortality and omniscience. As we see with the story of the Pharaoh in surah 79, Pharoah claims that he is God."

"In college there were many people who simply ruled out the possibility of their being a God using the theory of evolution as their evidence against any claims that there was one." Hamid interjected.

The sheik smiled.

"One of Allah's attributes is actually Al-Bari or, The Evolver. Islam does not rule out evolution. Allah subhanahu wa ta'ala makes it very plain that there are stages to creation. He is Al-khaliq – the creator, as well as the evolver. The fact that life has evolved from water was revealed to the prophet over fourteen hundred years ago. And Allah has Created every animal from water; of them are some creeping on their bellies; some walk on two legs; and some on four. Allah Creates what He wills: for sure Allah has

Power over all things. Surah twenty-four, verse forty-five.

"In Surah forty-one, verse eleven Allah speaks of the Big Bang. Stating that the heavens and earth were like smoke and he ordered them to come together willingly or unwillingly. He then shapes them proportionately.

"As far as evolution and Darwin, other men propagated the "Death of God" philosophy; men like Philipp Mainlander and Fred Nietzsche. Many scientists claim that God is a figment of man's imagination and that all of life is matter in motion, ambiguously answering what puts that matter in motion."

Hamid was learning a lot from his consultations with the sheik. Most importantly, he was regaining his inner peace and sense of direction with every solitary and congregational prayer he made.

Hamid's sisters were all grown and married now. Two lived in the states and the oldest was still living in Kabul with her husband, another wealthy Opium lord. Although Hamid knew it was smart to prepare for war even in times of peace, he just wanted to enjoy himself and the presence of his family. He completely wrote off the feud between him and Wally. His plans were to forget about the whole thing and start fresh. Those plans were spoiled though when he got word that Ali had been murdered. He had been shot once in the head. Salaam told him that the maggots were already eating at his flesh when his body was discovered.

Hamid had to make the trip back to Buffalo to watch his last real companion be buried.

XXVIII

It didn't take Wally and Dumare long at all to get acclimated to the drug scene in Denver, Colorado. After they both financed homes, and Wally got a new set of wheels, a Buick Century for inconspicuousness. Slowly they began to venture out into the city of Denver and network.

One night at a club they ran into a guy named Dee. A local gunslinger, who resembled Rosco in every shape, form, and fashion. He was crazy but of good use. He introduced Wally and Dumare to a Mexican named Pedro. Supposedly Pedro had weight and though they knew it wouldn't t compare to what they were used to seeing dealing with Ali, options were limited so they would have to make it work for the mean time. They both bought an eighth from him, it was good so they called him again. This time for two kilograms.

"Yo Wally. This work won't come back." Dumare said, staring down at the fraudulent batch of cocaine that just wouldn't cook up.

"What chu mean it won't come back?" Wally replied angrily while walking over to the stove.

"How much bake you put on it?"

"I'm throwin one on seven, just enough to bring it back."

"It might need more" Wally said.

After staring at the Pyrex jar's contents with much scrutiny like a chemist trying to locate the chemical imbalance, he conceded, they had gotten beat.

"Aight, just wrap the rest of it back up, we goin to see Papi right now, Yo Dee..." He called to the newest member of their team who was in the living room staring at the TV.

"Call Kev; tell em I need a favor."

Wally grabbed his MP5 and blew off the thin layer of dust it had collected in its brief time off of work. Its ninja black color perfectly matched the Kenneth Cole sweater he placed it beneath.

"Not until I say so this time." Wally warned Dee.

"None of that shit you pulled at the club, you could've got us jammed. No unnecessary shit."

"Alright, Alright..." Dee said, his eyes never leaving his twin Desert Eagles. He kissed one barrel then the other. Wally shook his head; he was bewildered by just how demented Dee really was.

At the sound of Kev's horn below, the three proceeded to leave Wally's stash apartment. Wally quickly wrapped the thick wool Andrew Marc scarf around his nose and mouth as the cold gust of December wind crashed into his face like a thousand ice-cycles being thrown at 100 miles an hour. Dee pulled the string on his hoody tight until nothing was visible but his cruel black eyes. Dumare just ran to the cab and jumped into the warmth of the back seat.

Heavy precipitation striking cold currents had the city streets covered in fluffy white snow, but a lack of respect and compensation could soon have that same white snow covered in warm red blood.

"Wussup yall?" Kev said before putting his taxi in drive. Kevin was a half-Indian, half-black cab driver who had drove for Wally on a few other occasions, he was down.

"Where we headed?" Kev asked as they pulled up to a stop sign at the end of the block. Wally let him know they were headed to Pedro's. Kev knew that address all too well, he had made plenty runs there. They headed that way carefully, the streets were slick with ice. Nothing else was said until they pulled up in front of Pedro's pad.

"Wait right here, Dumare told Kev, I don t care how long it takes, just wait!"

Wally, Dumare, and Dee exited the cab and walked briskly to the apartment building trying to escape the cold. Wally knocked on the door to the apartment Pedro was usually in. A shadow appeared at the bottom of the door and the peephole went completely black. The person behind the door stepped away for a second then suddenly the door flew open and a chrome barrel encompassing an ominous black hole stared directly at Wally. The infrared beam slightly below the barrel placed a small red dot right between Wally's eyebrows.

A look of surprise mixed with a hint of fear washed over Wally's face. Slightly behind the six-foot goon with ten too many tattoos, Wally could see Pedro standing right behind his bodyguard's right shoulder biting into the juicy, green flesh of a fresh avocado with a devious smile on his face.

"Yo Pedro, tell ya man to be easy." Wally said. Pedro gave Jorge an order in Spanish. Jorge lowered the cannon-sized .44 revolver he was holding and walked back into the apartment. Pedro's smile widened.

"Come in, come in." He said, as if the whole thing was one big joke. He knew he had a sick sense of humor and he could sense that Wally didn't appreciate the joke.

Being about three inches taller than Wally, Pedro put his arm around Wally's shoulder and ushered him into the apartment. Lucky for Wally, Pedro never felt the weapon beneath his coat.

Once again Pedro said something in Spanish; this time to the woman in the kitchen. She brought Wally, Dumare, and Dee drinks. Dee was the only one to accept.

Pedro began to bite into his avocado again when Wally said,

"What is this Papi?" He tossed the package he had gotten from Pedro on the table. Pedro stared aggressively at Wally then instantly rubbed his face vigorously, as if to massage from it the malevolent expression. He regretted showing aggression. He decided to be cordial.

"What's wrong with it?" He asked as nice as possible while examining the cocaine one the table.

"It won't rock up. Basically, you sold me some bad work and you can either compensate me with something real or you can reimburse me. One or the other."

Pedro looked furious.

"Don t you ever come in my home making demands or sending threats, accusing me of ripping you off."

By this time Pedro was standing with his finger pointed at Wally like a dictator making a speech.

"We got the best fish scale in this city. If you got beat then I got beat. But I don t have to beat anyone."

Pedro's demeanor was making Dee edgy. He tightened his grip on the guns beneath his hooded sweatshirt, saturating them in his anxious perspiration.

"But I like you Wally, you know that, so for the sake of our relationship, let's just whip it together, find out what is going on. Cool?"

"Yea, that's coo, let's whip it."

Pedro grabbed an empty jar from the cabinet and poured in a small amount of powder. He turned the gas stove on full blast. After placing the jar in a pot of water and placing the pot on top of the burner, the blue flames reached up and cradled the bottom of the silver pot. After the white powder melted down to oil, Pedro poured in a small amount of baking soda and whipped the mixture. After going through a bunch of culinary histrionics and realizing the coke was indeed bad, Pedro glanced at Jorge. His eyes told him to prepare for war. He wouldn't be able to repay Wally considering he had taken an even greater loss than Wally had.

At the same time Wally looked at Dee and Dumare and nodded his head. Without hesitation, Wally pulled the submachine gun from under his shirt and started spraying. Glass shattered and baking soda poured from a bullet hole in the Arm & Hammer box. Salma, Pedro's girlfriend screamed and bent down to kiss Pedro's cooling lips. She cradled his corpse like an infant child until Dee walked up behind her and shot her in the head. She slumped, dying with her lover in her arms. Dee laughed hysterically.

"Oh shit! You see that Wally? You see how her head split?"

Wally shook his head. The problem wasn't t being able to kill someone; it was being able to enjoy it. Dee loved it.

"D, check that room on the left." Wally told Dumare as they stepped over Jorge's dead body. By the time they had finished searching the apartment, they had over $175,000. Wally decided to leave the cocaine which wasn't worth much anyway.

Dee, Dumare, and Wally ran outside and to the cab. Kev looked nervous.

"What did you guys do?"

"Just get outta here!"

Kev floored the Taxi. Not even a block away from Pedro's pad Kevin's cab hit a patch of black ice and began to spin out of control. Kev tugged hard at the wheel but before he could get the car under control, he crashed hard into a telephone pole. The pole split on impact and the top half came crashing down on the roof. It hit so hard that it broke Kevin's neck, killing him immediately.

A police officer, who was parked at the next corner, had watched the whole accident in shock. He ran over to the cab in time to help Wally, who was crawling out of the car in pain, to his feet.

Wally had bloody cash plastered all over the inside of his coat and on his jeans. The cop shot him a suspicious look after noticing the money. Wally looked in the back seat where Dumare was laid out, dead, his glazed eyes still open with a thin line of blood running from the corner of his mouth. The cop's eyes followed Wally's to the two packages of powder that had burst open on the seat right next to Dee. He had grabbed the cocaine anyway. Dee was struggling for life.

The cop had seen all he needed to. He reached out to apprehend Wally and a shot went off. The officer dropped holding his neck. He died in a matter of seconds. Dee smiled, blood in his mouth, and then he too passed out. Wally shook his head. It was all too much. He quickly fled the scene.

XXIX

Buffalo, New York

Gray clouds hovered above the cemetery, threatening to burst open at any moment and fulfill the prediction of the weather forecaster who called for rain. Makita didn't go off on Wally the way she had at the hospital, but she still didn't speak to him. Wally figured it was her way of preventing herself from saying something she may soon regret.

Black suits, fedoras and trench coats was all Wally could see. The faces besides Curtis and his family were a blur to him. The blackness was depressing. Burying Dumare was harder than Wally had imagined. Seeing him in that coffin, then seeing them toss the dirt on top of him. Watching his mother's heart bleed and her eyes cry as she watched a part of herself being buried, only to be dug up in memories and dreams. She felt as though children were supposed to bury their parents, not the other way around. That was life's cycle. A mother gives life to her child and her child in turn gives her life, in the form of death. When it's time. She was not supposed to be burying her son. With that thought she let out a long, piercing howl-like cry that tore Wally's heart to shreds. Mascara mixed in her tears covered her swollen eyes and ran down over her

198

cheeks. She broke down to her knees and it would have been completely to the floor had it not been for her husband and her oldest son's support. They held her up and eventually helped her back to her feet.

As they helped her back up Wally, guilt-ridden walked away, his eyes brimming with tears. He couldn't take the sadness of the funeral any longer, especially being as though he felt he had caused all of the grief. He would have to visit Dumare's grave site at a later date, when he could be alone with his fallen comrade.

Wally made his way to his car through the damp grass, and maze of headstones. A drizzle had begun to fall from the sky and if he were superstitious, he would have thought Mrs. Makita had caused it, the earth cried in the form of rain. Wally stood at his car contemplating a lesson Mr. Curtis had taught him about precipitation and how it was caused by the son of man when he reached for the door handle and noticed a shadowy figure approaching him. He turned to see Curtis, who placed his hand on Wally's shoulder and asked him.

"Did you know what Dumare's name meant or even what his full name was?"

"I know it was like Alu, or Olu- Dumare but no, I never knew what it meant." Wally said honestly.

"His name was Oludamare; it's a Yoruban word that basically means consciousness, which is the source of all creation. Dumare, unfortunately returned to that essence early, Influence is only effective when accepted. He made the choice to do whatever he did to end up like this, I don't blame you, so you shouldn't blame you. I want you to know that you're still welcome in my house. I hate to say this but maybe the purpose of my son's life was to serve as a lesson for you, you know to save you from the same early grave he's now resting in. Study the signs Wally, don t let my son's death be in vain."

Wally dropped a tear and Curtis hugged him close.

"My door has always been open to you and I'm not about to close em on you now."

It felt like that was all the security Wally was looking for, he let out a long over-due cry. A cry that was caused by a deprived childhood, an antagonizing ambivalent love and hatred towards his mother, the death of every single person he held dear to his heart and his inability to prevent it. He felt powerless and it hurt. He cried because once again he had brought pain to Dumare's mother; a woman who had always been there for him, a mother when his biological one refused to be. He cried, and not just tears, a strained cry that came from deep in his stomach.

"It's alright Wally." Curtis said encouraging him to get it all out.

The rain had picked up dramatically now and they were both drenched. Wally was thinking at that moment, how could Curtis always remain so stoic; exert so much inner-strength, at times like these? The man always exhibited strength. It was because he accepted all seasons as they came, cherished the winter just as much as the spring and the rain just as much as the sunshine. He knew life was about positive and negative, they're codependent and he accepted both aspects of life equally. Wally realized he still had growing to do, he hated pain.

After wiping his tears away Wally asked Curtis,

"How do you experience pain and happiness the same way? I mean, it's like you at cha son's wake and you wearing the same face you would wear at his birthday, how do you maintain that calm?"

"A man's character isn't built on happiness alone, without pain his life isn't fulfilled. I read this book by Khalil Gibran called Tears and Laughter and I can't quote exactly what he said but I'll paraphrase this one passage. Basically, he said, He wouldn't trade his laughter for all the riches in the world, nor would he be content with converting his tears to calm. He said it was his wish to, he said his fervent hope, that his whole life on this earth forever be tears and laughter. Tears that purify the heart and reveal the secret and mystery of life, laughter that brings one closer to his fellow man, tears with which he joins the broken-hearted and laughter that symbolizes joy over our very existence.

You can't enjoy true happiness without knowing true pain. So, I accept them both as they come, knowing neither of them last forever, cherish the happy times, and learn from the sad ones, you understand where I'm comin from?"

Wally just stared up at Curtis with respect and admiration.

"Thanks Mr. C, you know, thanks for everything. You always been like a father to me and I want you to know I appreciate that. I wish there was some way I could repay you for all you've done for me."

"There is a way you could repay me Wally…" Curtis said, actually happy that Wally had made the offer.

"Aint no way I could repay you for all the things you did for me."

"Yes there is, now are you gonna listen or keep on with this defeatist attitude?"

"My bad." Wally said. He allowed Mr. Curtis to speak.

"You can repay me by getting out of that game right now. Just giving it up and avoiding that early grave. That's how you can repay me."

Wally didn't respond. He wanted to swear to Curtis that he would stop right now but he didn't for fear that would be a promise he may break. He didn't know what events the future held or how he would respond to those events. He could only promise Curtis that he would try as hard as possible. The funeral of his best friend made what Curtis was saying, seem that much more logical.

Curtis noticed the hesitation and took it for what it was, indecisiveness on Wally's part.

"Just think about it for me. And even if you don't quit right away, just know I'm always gonna love you Wally, you're a son to me. Nothing can change that. The emotional bond I have with you is just as strong as the biological one I had with Dumare."

"Thank you Mr. Curtis. I swear that means a lot to me."

"Before you go, just take this in and give it some thought. Your thoughts are mirrored back to you through the world around you. Whatever it is that your mind believes Wally, that is what will be experienced as reality to you. Because of that fact, you, like all of us, live in a world created totally by you. Now of course, your own individual mind doesn't create everything in the universal reality but your own existence is governed by the things you perceive as real and fake, good and bad, so on and so forth. As far as the universal reality that we are all subject to; well, you can't necessarily determine what happens to you, but you do determine what happens in you. You be in a state of peace and move like G.O.D., with Gomer Oz Dabar - wisdom, strength, and beauty."

XXX

Hamid stared down at Ali's mannequin-like face and suit that seemed too expensive for a corpse. For some reason however, Hamid could not concentrate on Ali, or the funeral. His mind continued to drift to Wally and the war they were engaged in; the war in his homeland of Afghanistan, his deceased wife Katrina and the baby that had died with her. In some form or another, his mind was on death and it was starting to plague his heart. It was all becoming too unbearable. The thoughts of Paradise and Hell began to arise; the thought of not being a good Muslim in the sight of Allah. He had missed so many salah over the course of his stay in Buffalo and wondered if he would be forgiven for the sins he continued to commit. He thought about sayings of the Prophet Muhammad. How he had spoken on all the sons of Adam being sinners, but the best of sinners being those who repented. He hadn't done so in so long.

After paying his respects to Ali, Hamid exchanged salutations with the rest of the funeral party and left before the body was lowered into the ground. Death was finally starting to sicken him and he didn't want to watch the internment of another friend. He headed to nearby Delaware Park where he walked aimlessly in an attempt to collect his scattered thoughts. Finally, realizing that it was almost time for the Asr or the afternoon prayer, Hamid decided to make salat in the middle of the park.

After focusing his eyes on the ground in the spot he would prostrate, he stated his intentions with his heart to make prayer, to humble himself before the Lord, and to perform four rakats in congruence with the Sunnah. After his intention was stated, he raised his hands to his head and said in a moderate tone,

"Allahu Akbar - God is the greatest."

Folding his hands, right above left, over his naval he began to say the *Thana* in Arabic.

"Holy are you, O Allah, the praise worthy, and blessed is your name, and exalted is your majesty. And there is none to be worshipped besides you."

Next was *Tawwudh.*

"I seek refuge with Allah, from Satan, the rejected."

Then he recited Al-Fatihah.

"In the name of Allah, Most gracious most merciful, praise be to Allah, the lord of all the worlds; most gracious, most merciful; master of the Day of Judgment. Thee alone do we worship and thee alone do we beseech for help, guide us to the right path, the path of those on whom thy has bestowed thine blessings, but not those who have incurred thy displeasure nor of those who have gone astray."

Hamid continued the rest of his prayer and sat on a nearby bench. He felt a sereneness he hadn't felt in a very long time. A tranquility he felt could only be bestowed on a person by the almighty creator. The rain did not even bother him at this point as he thought about a verse in the Qur'an that made the rain a thing to be enjoyed.

"It is He who sends down rain from the skies: with it We produce vegetation of all kinds: from some we produce green (crops), out of which We produce grain, heaped (at harvest); out of the date-palm and its sheaths (or spathes) come clusters of dates hanging low and near and (then there are) gardens of grapes, and olives, and pomegranates, each similar in kind yet different in variety: when they begin to bear fruit, feast your eyes with fruit and their ripeness. Behold! In these things there are signs for people who believe."

After reciting the verse from the Qur'an, Hamid was inspired to pray again.

As Wally walked through the park, allowing the rain to wash over him as if washing away his sins, he took notice to a man who seemed to be praying, in the Islamic Fashion, near a tree. The man had bowed, rose up, raised his hands to the sides of his head, and then placed his forehead on the ground. The act grabbed Wally's attention and Wally was in awe by the act of obedience. It almost made him want to pray especially after all Curtis had said to him. Maybe he had created the wrong reality for himself. Maybe the reality he had created was in all actuality just a big illusion. Money had become his God. He had no religion outside of a sincere devotion to the streets and the drug game it cultivated. He had never bowed to anything and here this man had planted his forehead on wet grass to show submission to the Lord he served. Hamid began to admire the man.

The Man made a motion, turning his head to the right then the left. When the man's head turned towards the left, which was the direction from which Wally was watching him, Wally's heart drummed violently. The face...was...it was the face of his enemy...the face of Serenity and Rosco's killer. It was Hamid.

Wally turned and ran back to his car. He grabbed his pistol from beneath his seat. He pulled the top back to check the chamber. The copper of a bullet shimmered. He let the top click back in place. Wally tucked the chrome Nine-millimeter in his pants and walked back to where Hamid was now sitting.

Wally got within ten feet and pulled the pistol from his waist. Hamid spun around just in time. Like a hunted prey he hadn't seen Wally approaching, only sensed him as some internal feeling let him know danger was approaching and a predator was near. Wally fired three shots at Hamid's face. Hamid hit the ground after the third shot. The third bullet had torn through the skin on his face but hadn't penetrated the skull. He was still alive.

"Praise be to Allah". Said Hamid's pounding heart.

Wally was having trouble keeping his eyes open with all the rain. He walked over to Hamid who was still face down and stood over top of him. Pointing the gun at the back of Hamid's head, Wally squeezed the trigger. Just as he had pulled the trigger back, Hamid flipped over and shot up at Wally. Wally's bullet hit the mud and planted itself in the earth. Hamid's bullet landed in the right side of Wally's chest. Wally was rocked by the impact. He took a long, strained breath and backed up, still firing.

Hamid was now on his feet, firing at Wally in return. Hamid's face was covered in blood. A dark red, wet spot began to grow larger and larger on Wally's shirt beneath his jacket. Hamid was shot but Wally was hurt worse. His gun had been emptied. Moving slower and slower, he fell backwards, laid out, flat on his back. His chest was heaving. He was losing a lot of blood. His consciousness began to fade. He felt the end approaching.

It was now Hamid's turn to finish his foe off. He now stood over Wally. He pointed his gun at Wally s forehead. Then, the words of the Prophet began to resonate in his heart in mind.

"Whoever suppresseth his anger, when he hath in his power to show it, God will give him a great reward..."

What a bad time for morality to kick in. Still, a shot went off. Hamid turned his head to see who it was. Wally looked to the side as well, surprised but happy to still be alive.

A police officer, who had been in the area and heard the gunshots, was screaming something that the rain was making it hard to hear. His gun was pointed at the sky then towards Hamid. Hamid shot in the cop's direction then turned back towards Wally. When he looked down Wally was gone. He looked and saw Wally running away. He resembled a wounded animal and though Hamid could have hit him from where he was, he didn't. He allowed Wally to run and even hoped that he made it away from the police officers. Instead, he turned towards the officer and emptied his clip. He wasn't t trying to kill the cop, just get him to retreat so that he could get away. Once his gun was empty, he ran towards his car.

Wally looked up at Hamid as he shot at the cop. He had to get away. He was not about to die right now. Somehow, through all the immense pain in his chest and the numbness of his legs, he found the strength to run. He swore to himself that he wouldn't stop running until he was on an island somewhere far away from all the madness, he had found himself in. The Buffalo police force had a different plan however. Just as Wally made it to his car, red and blue lights were coming directly at him while police sirens blared. Wally's eyes opened wide with nervousness as the squad car pulled right in front of him. Wally jumped in his car...the cop hopped out of his...Wally started the engine...the cop aimed his gun at Wally...

Hamid walked quickly towards his car. For some reason the cop was after Wally and hadn't chased him. Somewhere he had lost him. The officer had chased Wally with vigor, something he no longer had the energy, will, or want to do.

Hamid was headed straight to the airport and back to Afghanistan; home; where he belonged. It seemed to be a smooth getaway then just as he approached Buffalo s International Airport, the deafening sound of sirens made Hamid s heart drop. Reluctantly he looked in his rearview mirror. Three police cruisers, in hot pursuit.

Ω

The Epilogue

"My whole body hurts, the morphine is helpin a lil bit, but surgery was rough. They had to remove one of my lungs and my appendix. I can just imagine it. My whole torso was probably open, nasty incision; that's gonna leave a nasty scar. It's cold as hell in this room, I have nothing on under this apron but some draws they put on me, that and these tubes, I got a catheter going into my...shh, I don't even want to think it. I'm dizzy from the medicine and I just wanna sleep; but now that I'm awake, I can't... I lost everything man, I mean, I survived, and I'm thankful to still be alive, but what good is livin' when you lose everything you love?

I lost Serenity, the only woman I ever loved, who I still love with all my heart. I lost my best friend, my hard headed cousin, and in the end, what was it worth? I have to live the rest of my life with one lung and all kinds of respiratory problems that's gonna stem from stress that's gonna be placed on the lung I have left, cause it's gonna have to compensate for the missing one, I have no appendix. The doctor said I don't need it, but I don't know, it wasn't there for no reason...My mom is gone. Them years of drug

211

abuse caught up with her, it happened while I was in Denver but Mr. Curtis just told me about it yesterday. Apparently, she took one too many blasts, weak heart couldn't take it anymore. She had a heart attack, went into cardiac arrest, somethin' like that. I didn't even get to go see her. I'm not surprised it happened, matter'fact I kinda expected it to. I wasn't callin' her a zombie for no reason. She literally operated on crack and free base like a car does on gas, without it she wouldn't run. Her body was flooded with it until she couldn't function without it. I mean that literally. I saw this zombie movie called Dawn of the dead, and these zombies used to walk around, eyes wide open, lookin' and smellin' like death, lookin for humans to feed on. Nothin' else mattered to them but getting' that human blood and flesh. It was the same with her; that's where the name came from.

I look at it now, though and I feel a lil' guilty, no matter what, no matter how tough I used to act, or how I used to pretend her condition didn't bother me. It did, it used to make me so sad, but my sadness always turned to anger. She was my mom though, like, you only get one of them... Here I go cryin', I said I wasn't gonna cry... It's har... It's hard though. When I was a baby, it was different, we had real good times together, me, her, and my dad, it was better back then. But he got murdered, and then that crack epidemic hit and look; My mom, Serenity's mom, Rosco's mom, all of 'em, strung out, then I'm in a war with somebody I don't even know, somebody from clear across the world. I don't even know this man but we were at each other like animals; and for what? For what? I mean, I know why on the surface level, Rosco killed his man, but over what? We all scramblin' in this drug game, that's ten times bigger than us. I don't even know that man, still don't...

Was it worth it? Is it ever worth it? While you makin money it may seem like it, but the whole time you throwin' rocks at the penitentiary, and them rocks is addin' up, and then they get ya ass, when them feds drop them 848's when you get your paper work and it say you versus the United States of America, when they get you in that federal courtroom, they gon' hit you for every single rock, stone, and pebble you threw at they pens, believe me. And you either gon' bite it, or you gon' do what rats do when they caught in a trap, anything to get out of that trap, even if that means bitin' their own leg off to get loose. Or you might just find yourself in front of a barrel. And you know what's comin' next. I was just a pawn man, a pawn...I don't know what happen wit ol' boy, the Arab I don't even care, that shit is over for me. Mr. C said when I heal up, and they let me outta this hospital he got somethin' set up for me. I think I'ma take him up on his offer. I think I'm done with this game. But for now, while I heal, I'ma try to find GOD."

    Hamid started intently at the TV. CNN was airing a special on America's "War on Drugs". One thing Hamid found amusing about American media was its hypocrisy and how little they tried to disguise it. Still, he listened closely because after the talks of cocaine they would be talking about Afghanistan and its high levels of cultivation in poppy plants.

"Well, I think back to 1982," One reporter said, *"when President Regan formally declared his administration's war on drugs. At that time eighty to ninety percent of the nation's cocaine was entering through south Florida, ten to fifteen percent through Southern California and the rest of the southwest border and the federal government met the challenge head on. They established the South Florida Task Force and placed then, Vice President George Bush Sr. in charge.*

"The DEA was reinforced in Miami with seventy-three additional agents, the FBI forty-three more; U.S Customs was reinforced with one hundred and forty-five more investigators, and so on down the line with the U.S Border Patrol, the Bureau of Alcohol, Tobacco and Firearms, etcetera. The Coast guard was strengthened with faster cutters, and the U.S Navy pitched in with its E2C "Hawkeye" surveillance aircraft , I mean just think about it, at that time money was no object as far as the war on drugs was concerned, even local Florida state law enforcement intensified their efforts under the supervisory umbrella of the task force. It worked Jim, " The reporter said enthusiastically.

"From 1982, when this task force began operations, a kilo of cocaine cost and estimated $47,000 to about $60,000 in Miami. Today that cost has dropped dramatically to about $20,000 to $25,000. And we are still world's biggest market for narcotics. We count for only five percent of the world's populations but consume an estimated seventy-five percent of the world's cocaine supply. Something is terribly wrong."

Another reporter chimed in.

"And if you remember, November 18, 1988 President Reagan signed and Anti-Drug Abuse Act that grandly stated "It is the declared policy of the United States Government to create a drug-free America by 1955".

Hamid just laughed,
"Don't these fools realize what America would stand to lose if they completely destroyed the drug trade. It's a billion-dollar operation, one that they eat off of..." He shook his head at what he viewed as naivety as its best while the first reporter began to speak again.

"I don't think any American President made the purging of the drug crisis as big a priority as President Bush. If you think back to his inaugural

address in 1989, he very confidently asserted, 'Take my word for it, this scourge will stop!'"

The men went on and on about the cocaine problem in America. It sounded dull to Hamid. He knew that these types of shows were to put the public at ease, nothing more or less. They weren't meant to be taken seriously, because the American government wasn't serious about eradicating drugs in this country but maybe they were serious about Afghanistan. Hamid's homeland was an enemy of America's and as long as they were the world's biggest producer of opium, they were a problem because they would have money and resources. They were already establishing their democracy in Iraq and taking control of the oil there so it didn't surprise Hamid when at the bottom of the screen he saw:

"UN Anti-drug Chief says opium Industry must be destroyed and a war must be waged against these drug barons"

Hamid was born in Helmand so he already knew that it was the biggest opium producer in Afghanistan. It didn't surprise him to hear that only 6 of the 34 provinces in Afghanistan were opium-free, how 50 percent of Afghanistan's GDP or Gross Domestic Product is opium and that opium cultivation rose 59 percent in 2006.

He laughed to himself when they questioned Muslims who explained that selling drugs was

Haram, which means forbidden, in Islam. Yet, he felt a deep anger inside of himself as he realized that like Wally, he had been played like a dummy. The top people sat back and got rich, while the bottom-feeders ran wild, killing each other in the streets for crumbs.

Well, as he glanced around the interior of the Federal Penitentiary he would reside in for the rest of his life, he realized he had the rest of his existence to contemplate how foolishly he had been trapped into a vicious game where he had been a mere piece, and the government had been the real players. For now, The Maghrib prayer was coming in. It was time to pray to GOD.

"That's the irony of living, you never realize the truth until it's too late, and a lot of good the truth does when you're an old man and the game is over."
-Sam Giancana

www.ingramcontent.com/pod-product-compliance
Lightning Source LLC
Chambersburg PA
CBHW070820120626
46556CB00002B/595